Many years ago Agatha Christie
wrote two novels for posthumous
publication: *Curtain*, Hercule
Poirot's last case, and *Sleeping
Murder*, in which Miss Jane Marple
now makes her final appearance.

And so this book is a double farewell, first to Dame Agatha, one of
the greatest mystery writers of all
time, and second to that universally
beloved spinster, Miss Jane Marple.

SLEEPING MURDER

"Displays Agatha Christie's personal sense of
what she calls 'evil,' of murder as an affront
and a violation and an act of unique cruelty
. . . It is certainly the most interesting aspect
of her personality and probably accounts for
her extraordinary success."
—*The New York Times Book Review*

Bantam Books by Agatha Christie
Ask your bookseller for the books you have missed

SLEEPING MURDER

Agatha Christie

BANTAM BOOKS
TORONTO · NEW YORK · LONDON · SYDNEY

ᗒ

SLEEPING MURDER

*A Bantam Book / published by arrangement with
Dodd, Mead & Company*

PRINTING HISTORY

Dodd, Mead edition published September 1976
2nd printing ____ September 1976
3rd printing ____ September 1976
Literary Guild edition published December 1976
Serialized in the LADIES HOME JOURNAL, July and August 1976

Bantam edition / August 1977

2nd printing ____ August 1977	6th printing ____ January 1978
3rd printing _ September 1977	7th printing ____ November 1978
4th printing _ September 1977	8th printing ____ March 1980
5th printing ____ October 1977	9th printing ____ January 1981
10th printing ____ August 1981	

Cover painting by Tom Adams.

ISBN 0-553-20435-1

PRINTED IN THE UNITED STATES OF AMERICA

19 18 17 16 15 14 13

SLEEPING
MURDER

1

A Mouse

Gwenda Reed stood, shivering a little, on the quayside.

The docks and the custom sheds and all of England that she could see were gently waving up and down.

And it was in that moment that she made her decision—the decision that was to lead to such very momentous events.

She wouldn't go by the boat train to London as she had planned.

After all, why should she? No one was waiting for her, nobody expected her. She had only just got off that heaving, creaking boat (it had been an exceptionally rough three days through the Bay and up to Plymouth) and the last thing she wanted was to get into a heaving, swaying train. She would go to a hotel, a nice firm, steady hotel standing on good solid ground. And she would get into a nice steady bed that didn't creak and roll. And she would go to sleep, and the next morning—why, of course—what a splendid idea! She would hire a car and she would drive slowly and without hurrying herself all through the South of England looking about for a house—a nice house—the house that she and Giles had planned she should find. Yes, that was a splendid idea.

In that way she would see something of England—of the England that Giles had told her about and which she had never seen; although, like most New Zealanders, she called it home. At the moment, England was not looking particularly attractive. It was a grey day with rain imminent and a sharp, irritating wind blowing. Plymouth, Gwenda thought, as she moved forward obediently in the queue for Passports and Customs, was probably not the best of England.

On the following morning, however, her feelings were entirely different. The sun was shining. The view from her window was attractive. And the universe in general was no longer waving and wobbling. It had steadied down. This was England at last and here she was, Gwenda Reed, young married woman of twenty-one, on her travels. Giles's return to England was uncertain. He might follow her in a few weeks. It might be as long as six months. His suggestion had been that Gwenda should precede him to England and should look about for a suitable house. They both thought it would be nice to have, somewhere, a permanency. Giles's job would always entail a certain amount of travelling. Sometimes Gwenda would come too, sometimes the conditions would not be suitable. But they both liked the idea of having a home—some place of their very own. Giles had inherited some furniture from an aunt recently, so that everything combined to make the idea a sensible and practical one.

Since both Gwenda and Giles were reasonably well-off, the prospect presented no difficulties.

Gwenda had demurred at first to choosing a house on her own. "We ought to do it together," she had said. But Giles had said laughingly: "I'm not much of a hand at houses. If *you* like it, *I* shall. A bit of a garden, of course, and not some brand-new horror—and not too big. Somewhere on the south coast was my idea. At any rate, not too far inland."

"Was there any particular place?" Gwenda asked. But Giles said No. He'd been left an orphan young (they were both orphans) and had been passed around to various relations for holidays, and no particular spot had any particular association for him. It was to be Gwenda's house, and as for waiting until they could choose it together, suppose he were held up for six months? What would Gwenda do with herself all that time? Hang about in hotels? No, she was to find a house and get settled in.

"What you mean is," said Gwenda, "do all the work!"

But she liked the idea of finding a home and having it all ready, cosy and lived in, for when Giles came back.

They had been married just three months and she loved him very much.

After sending for breakfast in bed, Gwenda got up and arranged her plans. She spent a day seeing Plymouth, which she enjoyed, and on the following day she hired a comfortable Daimler car and chauffeur and set off on her journey through England.

The weather was good and she enjoyed her tour very much. She saw several possible residences in Devonshire but nothing that she felt was exactly right. There was no hurry. She would go on looking. She learned to read between the lines of the house agents' enthusiastic descriptions and saved herself a certain number of fruitless errands.

It was on a Tuesday evening about a week later that the car came gently down the curving hill road into Dillmouth and on the outskirts of that still charming seaside resort, passed a For Sale board where, through the trees, a glimpse of a small white Victorian villa could be seen.

Immediately Gwenda felt a throb of appreciation—almost of recognition. This was *her* house! Already she was sure of it. She could picture the garden, the long windows —she was sure that the house was just what she wanted.

It was late in the day, so she put up at the Royal Clarence Hotel and went to the house agents whose name she had noted on the board the following morning.

Presently, armed with an order to view, she was standing in the old-fashioned long drawing room with its two French windows giving onto a flagged terrace in front of which a kind of rockery interspersed with flowering shrubs fell sharply to a stretch of lawn below. Through the trees at the bottom of the garden the sea could be seen.

"This is *my* house," thought Gwenda. "It's *home*. I feel already as though I know every bit of it."

The door opened and a tall melancholy woman with a cold in the head entered sniffing. "Mrs. Hengrave? I have an order from Messrs. Galbraith and Penderley. I'm afraid it's rather early in the day—" Mrs. Hengrave, blowing her nose, said sadly that that didn't matter at all. The tour of the house began.

Yes, it was just right. Not too large. A bit old-fashioned, but she and Giles could put in another bathroom or two. The kitchen could be modernized. It already had a stove fortunately. With a new sink and up-to-date equipment—

Through all Gwenda's plans and pre-occupations, the voice of Mrs. Hengrave droned thinly on recounting the details of the late Major Hengrave's last illness. Half of Gwenda attended to making the requisite noises of condolence, sympathy and under-standing. Mrs. Hengrave's people all lived in Kent—anxious she should come and settle near them . . . the Major had been very fond of Dillmouth, secretary for many years of the golf club, but she herself . . .

"Yes . . . Of course . . . Dreadful for you . . . Most natural . . . Yes, nursing homes *are* like that . . . Of course . . . You must be. . . ."

And the other half of Gwenda raced along in thought:

"Linen cupboard here, I expect . . . Yes. Double room—nice view of the sea—Giles will like that. Quite a useful little room here —Giles might have it as a dressing room . . . Bathroom—I expect the bath has a mahogany surround—Oh yes, it *has!* How lovely— and standing in the middle of the floor! I shan't change *that*—it's a period piece!"

Such an enormous bath!

One could have apples on the surround. And sailboats—and painted ducks. You could pretend you were in the sea . . . "I know, we'll make that dark back spare room into a couple

of really up-to-date green and chromium
bathrooms—the pipes ought to be all right
over the kitchen—and keep this just as it
is. . . ."

"Pleurisy," said Mrs. Hengrave. "Turning
to double pneumonia on the third day—"

"Terrible," said Gwenda. "Isn't there
another bedroom at the end of this passage?"

There was—and it was just the sort of
room she had imagined it would be—almost
round, with a big bow window. She'd have to
do it up, of course. It was in quite good condition, but why were people like Mrs. Hengrave so fond of that mustard-cum-biscuit
shade of wall paint?

They retraced their steps along the cor-
ridor. Gwenda murmured conscientiously,
"Six, no, seven bedrooms, counting the little
one and the attic."

The boards creaked faintly under her feet.
Already she felt that it was she and not Mrs.
Hengrave who lived here! Mrs. Hengrave
was an interloper—a woman who did up the
rooms in mustard-cum-biscuit colour and
liked a frieze of wisteria in her drawing
room. Gwenda glanced down at the type-
written paper in her hand on which the details of the property and the price asked were
given.

In the course of a few days Gwenda had
become fairly conversant with house values.

The sum asked was not large—of course the house needed a certain amount of moderniza- tion—but even then. . . . And she noted the words "Open to offer." Mrs. Hengrave must be very anxious to go to Kent and live near "her people."

They were starting down the stairs when quite suddenly Gwenda felt a wave of irra- tional terror sweep over her. It was a sicken- ing sensation, and it passed almost as quickly as it came. Yet it left behind it a new idea.

"The house isn't—haunted, is it?" de- manded Gwenda.

Mrs. Hengrave, a step below, and having just got to the moment in her narrative when Major Hengrave was sinking fast, looked up in an affronted manner.

"Not that I am aware of, Mrs. Reed. Why —has anyone—been saying something of the kind?"

"You've never felt or seen anything your- self? Nobody's *died* here?"

Rather an unfortunate question, she thought a split second of a moment too late, because presumably Major Hengrave—

"My husband died in the St. Monica's Nursing Home," said Mrs. Hengrave stiffly.

"Oh, of course. You told me so."

Mrs. Hengrave continued in the same rather glacial manner:

"In a house which was presumably built

about a hundred years ago; there would normally be deaths during that period. Miss Elworthy, from whom my dear husband acquired this house seven years ago, was in excellent health, and indeed planning to go abroad and do missionary work, and she did not mention any recent demises in her family."

Gwenda hastened to soothe the melancholy Mrs. Hengrave down. They were now once more in the drawing room. It was a peaceful and charming room, with exactly the kind of atmosphere that Gwenda coveted. Her momentary panic just now seemed quite incomprehensible. What *had* come over her? There was nothing wrong with the house.

Asking Mrs. Hengrave if she could take a look at the garden, she went out through the French windows onto the terrace.

"There should be steps here," thought Gwenda, "going down to the lawn."

But instead there was a vast uprising of forsythia which at this particular place seemed to have got above itself and effectually shut out all view of the sea.

Gwenda nodded to herself. She would alter all that.

Following Mrs. Hengrave, she went along the terrace and down some steps at the far side onto the lawn. She noted that the rockery was neglected and overgrown, and that most of the flowering shrubs needed pruning.

Mrs. Hengrave murmured apologetically that the garden had been rather neglected. Only able to afford a man twice a week. And quite often *he* never turned up.

They inspected the small but adequate kitchen garden and returned to the house. Gwenda explained that she had other houses to see, and that though she liked Hillside (what a commonplace name!) very much, she could not decide immediately.

Mrs. Hengrave parted from her with a somewhat wistful look and a last long-lingering sniff.

Gwenda returned to the agents, made a firm offer subject to the surveyor's report, and spent the rest of the morning walking round Dillmouth. It was a charming and old-fashioned little seaside town. At the far, "modern" end, there were a couple of new-looking hotels and some raw-looking bungalows, but the geographical formation of the coast with the hills behind had saved Dillmouth from undue expansion.

After lunch Gwenda received a telephone call from the agents saying that Mrs. Hengrave accepted her offer. With a mischievous smile on her lips Gwenda made her way to the post office and despatched a cable to Giles.

HAVE BOUGHT A HOUSE. LOVE. GWENDA.

"That'll tickle him up," said Gwenda to herself. "Show him that the grass doesn't grow under *my* feet!"

2

Wallpaper

A month had passed and Gwenda had moved
into Hillside. Giles's aunt's furniture had
come out of storage and was arranged round
the house. It was good-quality old-fashioned
stuff. One or two overlarge wardrobes
Gwenda had sold, but the rest fitted in
nicely and was in harmony with the house.
There were small gay papier-mâché tables
in the drawing room, inlaid with mother of
pearl and painted with castles and roses.
There was a prim little worktable with a
gathered sack underneath of puce silk, there
was a rosewood bureau and a mahogany sofa
table.

The so-called easy chairs Gwenda had
relegated to various bedrooms and had
bought two large squashy wells of comfort
for herself and Giles to stand at each side of
the fireplace. The large Chesterfield sofa
was placed near the windows. For curtains

Gwenda had chosen old-fashioned chintz of pale eggshell blue with prim urns of roses and yellow birds on them. The room, she now considered, was exactly right.

She was hardly settled yet, since she had workmen in the house still. They should have been out by now, but Gwenda rightly estimated that until she herself came into residence, they would not go.

The kitchen alterations were finished, the new bathrooms nearly so. For further decorating Gwenda was going to wait a while. She wanted time to savour her new home and decide on the exact colour schemes she wanted for the bedrooms. The house was really in very good order and there was no need to do everything at once.

In the kitchen a Mrs. Cocker was now installed, a lady of condescending graciousness, inclined to repulse Gwenda's over-democratic friendliness, but who, once Gwenda had been satisfactorily put in her place, was willing to unbend.

On this particular morning Mrs. Cocker deposited a breakfast tray on Gwenda's knees as she sat up in bed.

"When there's no gentleman in the house," Mrs. Cocker affirmed, "a lady prefers her breakfast in bed." And Gwenda had bowed to this supposedly English enactment.

"Scrambled this morning," Mrs. Cocker observed, referring to the eggs. "You said something about finnan haddock, but you wouldn't like it in the bedroom. It leaves a smell. I'm giving it to you for your supper, creamed on toast."

"Oh, thank you, Mrs. Cocker."

Mrs. Cocker smiled graciously and prepared to withdraw.

Gwenda was not occupying the big double bedroom. That could wait until Giles returned. She had chosen instead the end room, the one with the rounded walls and the bow window. She felt thoroughly at home in it and happy.

Looking round her now, she exclaimed impulsively:

"I do like this room."

Mrs. Cocker looked round indulgently.

"It is quaite a naice room, madam, though small. By the bars on the window I should say it had been the nursery at one time."

"I never thought of that. Perhaps it has."

"Ah, well," said Mrs. Cocker, with implication in her voice, and withdrew.

"Once we have a gentleman in the house," she seemed to be saying, "who knows? A nursery *may* be needed."

Gwenda blushed. She looked round the room. A nursery? Yes, it would be a nice nursery. She began furnishing it in her mind. A big doll's house there against the wall. And low cupboards with toys in them. A fire burning cheerfully in the grate and a tall guard round it with things airing on the rail. But not this hideous mustard wall. No, she would have a gay wallpaper. Something bright and cheerful. Little bunches of poppies alternating with bunches of cornflowers. . . . Yes, that would be lovely. She'd try and find a wallpaper like that. She felt sure she had seen one somewhere.

One didn't need much furniture in the room. There were two built-in cupboards, but one of them, a corner one, was locked and the key lost. Indeed the whole thing had been painted over, so that it could not have been opened for many years. She must get the men to open it up before they left. As it was, she hadn't got room for all her clothes.

She felt more at home every day in Hillside. Hearing a throat being ponderously cleared and a short dry cough through the open window, she hurried over her breakfast. Foster, the temperamental jobbing gardener, who was not always reliable in his promises, must be here today as he had said he would be.

Gwenda bathed, dressed, put on a tweed skirt and a sweater and hurried out into the garden. Foster was at work outside the drawing-room window. Gwenda's first action had been to get a path made down through the rockery at this point. Foster had been recalcitrant, pointing out that the forsythia would have to go and the weigela, and them there lilacs, but Gwenda had been adamant, and he was now almost enthusiastic about his task.

He greeted her with a chuckle.

"Looks like you're going back to old times, miss." (He persisted in calling Gwenda "miss.")

"Old times? How?"

Foster tapped with his spade.

"I come on the old steps—see, that's where they went—just as you want 'em now. Then someone planted them over and covered them up."

"It was very stupid of them," said Gwenda. "You want a vista down to the lawn and the sea from the drawing-room window."

Foster was somewhat hazy about a vista—but he gave a cautious and grudging assent.

"I don't say, mind you, that it won't be an improvement. . . . Gives you a view—and them shrubs made it dark in the drawing room. Still they was growing a treat—never seen a healthier lot of forsythia. Lilacs isn't much, but them wiglers costs money—and mind you—they're too old to replant."

"Oh, I know. But this is much, much nicer."

"Well"—Foster scratched his head—"maybe it is."

"It's *right*," said Gwenda, nodding her head. She asked suddenly: "Who lived here before the Hengraves? They weren't here very long, were they?"

"Matter of six years or so. Didn't belong. Afore them? The Miss Elworthys. Very churchy folk. Low church. Missions to the heathen. Once had a black clergyman staying here, they did. Four of 'em there was, and their brother—but he didn't get much of a look-in with all those women. Before them —now let me see, it was Mrs. Findeyson— ah! she was the real gentry, she was. She belonged. Was living here afore I was born."

"Did she die here?" asked Gwenda.

"Died out in Egypt or some such place. But they brought her home. She's buried up to churchyard. She planted that magnolia and those labiurnams. And those pittispores. Fond of shrubs, she was."

Foster continued:

"Weren't none of those new houses built up along the hill then. Countrified it was. No cinema then. And none of them new shops. Or that there parade on the front." His tone held the disapproval of the aged for all innovations. "Changes," he said with a snort. "Nothing but changes."

"I suppose things are bound to change," said Gwenda. "And after all, there are lots of improvements nowadays, aren't there?"

"So they say. I ain't noticed them. Changes!" He gestured towards the macrocarpa hedge on the left through which the gleam of a building showed. "Used to be the Cottage Hospital, that used," he said. "Nice place and handy. Then they goes and builds a great place near to a mile out of town. Twenty minutes' walk if you want to get there on a visiting day—or three-pence on the bus." He gestured once more towards the hedge. "It's a girls' school now. Moved in ten years ago. Changes all the time. People takes a house nowadays and lives in it ten or twelve years and then off they goes. Restless. What's the good of that? You can't do any proper planting unless you can look well ahead."

Gwenda looked affectionately at the magnolia.

"Like Mrs. Findeyson," she said.

"Ah. She was the proper kind. Come here as a bride, she did. Brought up her children and married them, buried her husband, had her grandchildren down in the summers, and took off in the end when she was nigh on eighty."

Foster's tone held warm approval.

Gwenda went back into the house smiling a little.

She interviewed the workmen, and then returned to the drawing room, where she sat down at the desk and wrote some letters. Amongst the correspondence that remained to be answered was a letter from some cousins of Giles's who lived in London. Any time she wanted to come to London, they begged her to come and stay with them at their house in Chelsea.

Raymond West was a well-known (rather

than popular) novelist and his wife Joan, Gwenda knew, was a painter. It would be fun to go and stay with them, though probably they would think she was a most terrible Philistine. "Neither Giles nor I are a bit highbrow," reflected Gwenda.

A sonorous gong boomed pontifically from the hall. Surrounded by a great deal of carved and tortured black wood, the gong had been one of Giles's aunt's prized possessions. Mrs. Cocker herself appeared to derive distinct pleasure from sounding it, and always gave full measure. Gwenda put her hands to her ears and got up.

She walked quickly across the drawing room to the wall by the far window and then brought herself up short with an exclamation of annoyance. It was the third time she'd done that. She always seemed to expect to be able to walk through solid wall into the dining room next door.

She went back across the room and out into the front hall and then round the angle of the drawing-room wall and so along to the dining room. It was a long way round, and it would be annoying in winter, for the front hall was draughty and the only central heating was in the drawing room and dining room and two bedrooms upstairs.

"I don't see," thought Gwenda to herself as she sat down at the charming Sheraton dining table which she had just bought at vast expense in lieu of Aunt Lavender's massive square mahogany one, "I don't see why I shouldn't have a doorway made through from the drawing room to the dining room. I'll talk to Mr. Sims about it when he comes this afternoon."

Mr. Sims was the builder and decorator, a persuasive middle-aged man with a husky voice and a little notebook which he always held at the ready to jot down any expensive idea that might occur to his patrons.

Mr. Sims, when consulted, was keenly appreciative.

"Simplest thing in the world, Mrs. Reed— and a great improvement, if I may say so."

"Would it be very expensive?" Gwenda was by now a little doubtful of Mr. Sims's assents and enthusiasms. There had been a little unpleasantness over various extras not included in Mr. Sims's original estimate.

"A mere trifle," said Mr. Sims, his husky voice indulgent and reassuring. Gwenda looked more doubtful than ever. It was Mr. Sims's trifles that she had learnt to distrust. His straightforward estimates were studiously moderate.

"I'll tell you what, Mrs. Reed," said Mr. Sims coaxingly, "I'll get Taylor to have a look when he's finished with the dressing room this afternoon, and then I can give you an exact idea. Depends what the wall's like."

Gwenda assented. She wrote to Joan West thanking her for her invitation, but saying that she would not be leaving Dillmouth at present since she wanted to keep an eye on the workmen. Then she went out for a walk along the front and enjoyed the sea breeze. She came back into the drawing room, and Taylor, Mr. Sims's leading workman, straightened up from the corner and greeted her with a grin.

"Won't be no difficulty about this, Mrs. Reed," he said. "Been a door here before, there has. Somebody as didn't want it has just had it plastered over."

Gwenda was agreeably surprised. "How extraordinary," she thought, "that I've always seemed to feel there was a door there." She remembered the confident way she had walked to it at lunchtime. And remembering it, quite suddenly, she felt a tiny shiver of uneasiness. When you came to think of it, it was really rather odd. . . . Why should she have felt so sure that there was a door there? There was no sign of it on the outside wall. How had she guessed—known—that there was a door just there? Of course it would be convenient to have a door through to the dining room, but why had she always gone so unerringly to that one particular spot? Anywhere on the dividing wall would have done equally well, but she had always gone automatically, thinking of other things, to the one place where a door had actually been.

"I hope," thought Gwenda uneasily, "that I'm not clairvoyant or anything. . . ."

There had never been anything in the least psychic about her. She wasn't that kind of person. Or was she? That path outside from the terrace down through the shrubbery to the lawn. Had she in some way known it was there when she was so insistent on having it made in that particular place?

"Perhaps I am a bit psychic," thought Gwenda uneasily. "Or is it something to do with the house?"

Why had she asked Mrs. Hengrave that day if the house was haunted?

It wasn't haunted! It was a darling house! There couldn't be anything wrong with the house. Why, Mrs. Hengrave had seemed quite surprised by the idea.

Or had there been a trace of reserve, of wariness, in her manner?

"Good heavens, I'm beginning to imagine things," thought Gwenda.

She brought her mind back with an effort to her discussion with Taylor.

"There's one other thing," she added. "One of the cupboards in my room upstairs is stuck. I want to get it opened."

The man came up with her and examined the door.

"It's been painted over more than once,"

he said. "I'll get the men to get it open for you tomorrow, if that will do."

Gwenda acquiesced and Taylor went away.

That evening Gwenda felt jumpy and nervous. Sitting in the drawing room and trying to read, she was aware of every creak of the furniture. Once or twice she looked over her shoulder and shivered. She told herself repeatedly that there was nothing in the incident of the door and the path. They were just coincidences. In any case they were the result of plain common sense.

Without admitting it to herself, she felt nervous about going up to bed. When she finally got up and turned off the lights and opened the door into the hall, she found herself dreading to go up the stairs. She almost ran up them in her haste, hurried along the passage and opened the door of her room. Once inside she at once felt her fears calmed and appeased. She looked round the room affectionately. She felt safe in here—safe and happy. Yes, now she was here, she was safe. ("Safe from what, you idiot?" she asked herself.) She looked at her pyjamas spread out on the bed and her bedroom slippers below them.

"Really, Gwenda, you might be six years old! You ought to have bunny shoes, with rabbits on them."

She got into bed with a sense of relief and was soon asleep.

The next morning she had various matters to see to in the town. When she came back, it was lunchtime.

"The men have got the cupboard open in your bedroom, madam," said Mrs. Cocker as she brought in the delicately fried sole, the mashed potatoes and the creamed carrots.

"Oh, good," said Gwenda.

She was hungry and enjoyed her lunch. After having coffee in the drawing room, she went upstairs to her bedroom. Crossing the room, she pulled open the door of the corner cupboard.

Then she uttered a sudden frightened little cry and stood staring.

The inside of the cupboard revealed the original papering of the wall, which elsewhere had been done over in the yellowish wall paint. The room had once been gaily papered in a floral design, a design of little bunches of scarlet poppies alternating with bunches of blue cornflowers. . . .

Gwenda stood there staring a long time, then she went shakily over to the bed and sat down on it.

Here she was in a house she had never been in before, in a country she had never visited—and only two days ago she had lain in bed imagining a paper for this very room —and the paper she had imagined corresponded exactly with the paper that had once hung on the walls.

Wild fragments of explanation whirled round in her head. Donne, Experiment with Time—seeing forward instead of back . . .

She could explain the garden path and the connecting door as coincidence—but there couldn't be coincidence about this—you couldn't conceivably imagine a wallpaper of such a distinctive design and then find one exactly as you had imagined it. . . . No, there was some explanation that eluded her and that—yes, frightened her. Every now and then she was seeing, not forward, but back—back to some former state of the house. Any moment she might see something more—something she didn't want to see. . . . The house frightened her. . . . But was it the house or *herself?* She didn't want to be one of those people who *saw* things. . . .

She drew a long breath, put on her hat and coat and slipped quickly out of the house. At the post office she sent the following telegram:

WEST, 19 ADDWAY SQUARE CHELSEA LONDON. MAY I CHANGE MY MIND AND COME TO YOU TOMORROW.   GWENDA.

She sent it reply paid.

3

"Cover her face; mine eyes dazzle: she died young"

Raymond West and his wife did all they could to make young Giles's wife feel welcome. It was not their fault that Gwenda found them secretly rather alarming. Raymond, with his odd appearance, rather like a pouncing raven, his sweep of hair and his sudden crescendos of quite incomprehensible conversation, left Gwenda round-eyed and nervous. Both he and Joan seemed to talk a language of their own. Gwenda had never been plunged in a highbrow atmosphere before and practically all its terms were strange.

"We've planned to take you to a show or two," said Raymond while Gwenda was drinking gin and rather wishing she could have had a cup of tea after her journey.

Gwenda brightened up immediately.

"The ballet tonight at Sadler's Wells, and

26

tomorrow we've got a birthday party on for my quite incredible Aunt Jane—*The Duchess of Malfi* with Gielgud, and on Friday you simply must see *They Walked Without Feet*. Translated from the Russian—absolutely the most significant piece of drama for the last twenty years. It's at the little Witmore Theatre."

Gwenda expressed herself grateful for these plans for her entertainment. After all, when Giles came home, they would go together to the musical shows and all that. She flinched slightly at the prospect of *They Walked Without Feet*, but supposed she might enjoy it—only the point about "significant" plays was that you usually didn't.

"You'll adore my Aunt Jane," said Raymond. "She's what I should describe as a perfect Period Piece. Victorian to the core. All her dressing tables have their legs swathed in chintz. She lives in a village, the kind of village where nothing ever happens, exactly like a stagnant pond."

"Something did happen there once," his wife said drily.

Raymond waved his hand.

"A mere drama of passion—crude—no subtlety to it."

"You enjoyed it frightfully at the time," Joan reminded him with a slight twinkle.

"I sometimes enjoy playing village cricket," said Raymond with dignity.

"Anyway, Aunt Jane distinguished herself over that murder."

"Oh, she's no fool. She adores problems."

"Problems?" said Gwenda, her mind flying to arithmetic.

Raymond waved a hand.

"Any kind of problems. Why the grocer's wife took her umbrella to the church social on a fine evening. Why a gill of pickled shrimps was found where it was. What happened to the vicar's surplice. All grist to my Aunt Jane's mill. So if you've any problem in your life, put it to her, Gwenda. She'll tell you the answer."

He laughed and Gwenda laughed too, but not very heartily. She was introduced to Aunt Jane, otherwise Miss Marple, on the following day. Miss Marple was an attractive old lady, tall and thin, with pink cheeks and blue eyes, and a gentle, rather fussy manner. Her blue eyes often had a little twinkle in them.

After an early dinner at which they drank Aunt Jane's health, they all went off to His Majesty's theatre. Two extra men, an elderly artist and a young barrister, were in the party. The elderly artist devoted himself to Gwenda and the young barrister divided his attentions between Joan and Miss Marple, whose remarks he seemed to enjoy very much. At the theatre, however, this arrangement was reversed. Gwenda sat in the middle of the row between Raymond and the barrister.

The lights went down and the play began.

It was superbly acted and Gwenda enjoyed it very much. She had not seen very many first-rate theatrical productions.

The play drew to a close, came to that supreme moment of horror. The actor's voice came over the footlights filled with the tragedy of a warped and perverted mentality.

"Cover her face; mine eyes dazzle: she died young."

Gwenda screamed.

She sprang up from her seat, pushed blindly past the others out into the aisle, through the exit and up the stairs and so to the street. She did not stop, even then, but half walked, half ran, in a blind panic up the Haymarket.

It was not until she had reached Piccadilly that she noticed a free taxi cruising along, hailed it and, getting in, gave the address of the Chelsea house. With fumbling fingers she got out money, paid the taxi and went up the steps. The servant who let her in glanced at her in surprise.

"You've come back early, miss. Didn't you feel well?"

"I—no, yes—I—I felt faint."

"Would you like anything, miss? Some brandy?"

"No, nothing. I'll go straight up to bed."

She ran up the stairs to avoid further questions.

She pulled off her clothes, left them on the floor in a heap and got into bed. She lay there shivering, her heart pounding, her eyes staring at the ceiling.

She did not hear the sound of fresh arrivals downstairs, but after about five minutes the door opened and Miss Marple came in. She had two hot-water bottles tucked under her arm and a cup in her hand.

Gwenda sat up in bed, trying to stop her shivering.

"Oh, Miss Marple, I'm frightfully sorry. I don't know what— It was awful of me. Are they very annoyed with me?"

"Now don't worry, my dear child," said Miss Marple. "Just tuck yourself up warmly with these hot-water bottles."

"I don't really need a hot-water bottle."

"Oh yes, you do. That's right. And now drink this cup of tea."

It was hot and strong and far too full of sugar, but Gwenda drank it obediently. The shivering was less acute now.

"Just lie down now and go to sleep," said Miss Marple. "You've had a shock, you know. We'll talk about it in the morning. Don't worry about anything. Just go to sleep."

She drew the covers up, smiled, patted Gwenda and went out.

Downstairs Raymond was saying irritably to Joan:

"What on earth was the matter with the girl? Did she feel ill, or what?"

"My dear Raymond, I don't know, she just screamed! I suppose the play was a bit too macabre for her."

"Well, of course Webster is a bit grisly. But I shouldn't have thought—" He broke off as Miss Marple came into the room. "Is she all right?"

"Yes, I think so. She'd had a bad shock, you know."

"Shock? Just seeing an Elizabethan drama?"

"I think there must be a little more to it than that," said Miss Marple thoughtfully.

Gwenda's breakfast was sent up to her. She drank some coffee and nibbled a little piece of toast. When she got up and came downstairs, Joan had gone to her studio, Raymond was shut up in his workroom, and only Miss Marple was sitting by the window which had a view over the river; she was busily engaged in knitting.

She looked up with a placid smile as Gwenda entered.

"Good morning, my dear. You're feeling better, I hope."

"Oh yes, I'm quite all right. How could I make such an utter *idiot* of myself last night, I don't know. Are they—are they very mad with me?"

"Oh no, my dear. They quite understand."

"Understand what?"

Miss Marple glanced up over her knitting.

"That you had a bad shock last night." She added gently: "Hadn't you better tell me all about it?"

Gwenda walked restlessly up and down.

"I think I'd better go and see a psychiatrist or someone."

"There are excellent mental specialists in London, of course. But are you sure it is necessary?"

"Well—I think I'm going mad. . . . I *must* be going mad."

An elderly parlourmaid entered the room with a telegram on a salver which she handed to Gwenda.

"The boy wants to know if there's an answer, m'am?"

Gwenda tore it open. It had been retelegraphed on from Dillmouth. She stared at it for a moment or two uncomprehendingly, then screwed it into a ball.

"There's no answer," she said mechanically.

The maid left the room.

"Not bad news, I hope, dear?"

"It's Giles—my husband. He's flying home. He'll be here in a week."

Her voice was bewildered and miserable. Miss Marple gave a gentle little cough.

"Well—surely—that is very nice, isn't it?"

"Is it? When I'm not sure if I'm mad or not? If I'm mad, I ought never to have married Giles. And the house and everything. I can't go back there. Oh, I don't know what to do."

Miss Marple patted the sofa invitingly.

"Now suppose you sit down here, dear, and just tell me all about it."

It was with a sense of relief that Gwenda accepted the invitation. She poured out the whole story, starting with her first view of Hillside and going on to the incidents that had first puzzled her and then worried her.

"And so I got rather frightened," she ended. "And I thought I'd come up to London—get away from it all. Only, you see, I couldn't get away from it. It followed me. Last night—" She shut her eyes and gulped reminiscently.

"Last night?" prompted Miss Marple.

"I daresay you won't believe this," said Gwenda, speaking very fast. "You'll think I'm hysterical or queer or something. It happened quite suddenly, right at the end. I'd enjoyed the play. I'd never thought once of the house. And then it came—out of the blue —when he said those words—"

She repeated in a low, quivering voice:

"*Cover her face; mine eyes dazzle: she died young.*"

"I was back there—on the stairs, looking down on the hall through the banisters, and I saw her lying there. Sprawled out—dead. Her hair all golden and her face all—all *blue!* She was dead, strangled, and someone was saying those words in that same horrible, gloating way—and I saw his hands—grey, wrinkled—not hands—monkey's paws. . . . It was horrible, I tell you. She was dead. . . ."

Miss Marple asked gently:

"Who was dead?"

The answer came back quick and mechanical:

"Helen. . . ."

4

Helen?

For a moment Gwenda stared at Miss Marple, then she pushed back the hair from her forehead.

"Why did I say that?" she said. "Why did I say Helen? I don't know any Helen!"

She dropped her hands with a gesture of despair.

"You see," she said, "I'm mad! I imagine things! I go about seeing things that aren't there. First it was only wallpapers—but now it's dead bodies. So I'm getting worse."

"Now don't rush to conclusions, my dear—"

"Or else it's the *house*. The house is haunted—or bewitched or something. . . . I see things that have happened there—or else I see things that are going to happen there— and that would be worse. Perhaps a woman called Helen is going to be murdered there. . . . Only I don't see if it's the *house* that's

35

haunted why I should see these awful things when I am away from it. So I think really that it must be me that's going queer. And I'd better go and see a psychiatrist *at once*— this morning."

"Well, of course, Gwenda dear, you can always do that when you've exhausted every other line of approach, but I always think myself that it's better to examine the simplest and most commonplace explanations first. Let me get the facts quite clear. There were three definite incidents that upset you. A path in the garden that had been planted over but that you felt was there, a door that had been bricked up, and a wallpaper which you imagined correctly and in detail without having seen it? Am I right?"

"Yes."

"Well, the easiest, the most natural explanation would be that you *had* seen them before."

"In another life, you mean?"

"Well, no, dear. I meant in *this* life. I mean that they might be actual *memories*."

"But I've never been in England until a month ago, Miss Marple."

"You are quite sure of that, my dear?"

"Of course I'm sure. I've lived near Christchurch in New Zealand all my life."

"Were you born there?"

"No, I was born in India. My father was a British Army officer. My mother died a year or two after I was born and he sent me back to her people in New Zealand to bring up. Then he himself died a few years later."

"You don't remember coming from India to New Zealand?"

"Not really. I do remember, frightfully vaguely, being on a boat. A round window thing—a porthole, I suppose. And a man in white uniform with a red face and blue eyes and a mark on his chin—a scar, I suppose. He used to toss me up in the air and I remember being half frightened and half loving it. But it's all very fragmentary."

"Do you remember a nurse—or an ayah?"

"Not an ayah—Nannie. I remember Nannie because she stayed for some time—until I was five years old. She cut ducks out of paper. Yes, she was on the boat. She scolded me when I cried because the captain kissed me and I didn't like his beard."

"Now that's very interesting, dear, because you see you are mixing up two different voyages. In one, the captain had a beard and in the other he had a red face and a scar on his chin."

"Yes," Gwenda considered, "I suppose I must be."

"It seems possible to me," said Miss Marple, "that when your mother died, your father brought you to *England* with him first, and that you actually lived at this house, Hillside. You've told me, you know, that the house felt like home to you as soon as you got inside it. And that room you chose to sleep in, it was probably your nursery—"

"It *was* a nursery. There were bars on the windows."

"You see? It had this pretty gay paper of cornflowers and poppies. Children remember their nursery walls very well. I've always remembered the mauve irises on my nursery walls and yet I believe it was repapered when I was only three."

"And that's why I thought at once of the toys, the doll's house and the toy cupboards?"

"Yes. And the bathroom. The bath with the mahogany surround. You told me that you thought of sailing ducks in it as soon as you saw it."

Gwenda said thoughtfully:

"It's true that I seemed to know right away just where everything was—the kitchen and the linen cupboard. And that I kept thinking there was a door through from the drawing room to the dining room. But surely it's quite impossible that I should come to England and actually buy the identical house I'd lived in long ago?"

"It's not *impossible*, my dear. It's just a very remarkable coincidence—and remarkable coincidences do happen. Your husband wanted a house on the south coast, you were looking for one, and you passed a house that stirred memories, and attracted you. It was the right size and a reasonable price and so you bought it. No, it's not too wildly improbable. Had the house been merely what is called (perhaps rightly) a haunted house, you would have reacted quite differently, I think. But you had no feeling of violence or repulsion except, so you have told me, at one very definite moment, and that was when you were just starting to come down the staircase and looking down into the hall."

Some of the scared expression came back into Gwenda's eyes.

She said:

"You mean—that—that Helen—that *that's* true too?"

Miss Marple said very gently:

"Well, I think so, my dear. . . . I think we must face the position that if the other things are memories, *that* is a memory too. . . ."

"That I really saw someone killed—strangled—and lying there dead?"

"I don't suppose you knew consciously that she was strangled. That was suggested by the play last night and fits in with your adult recognition of what a blue convulsed face must mean. I think a very young child, creeping down the stairs, would realize violence and death and evil and associate them with a certain series of words—for I think there's no doubt that the murderer actually *said* those words. It would be a very severe shock to a child. Children are odd little creatures. If they are badly frightened, especially by something they don't understand, they don't talk about it. They bottle it up. Seemingly, perhaps, they forget it. But the memory is still there deep down."

Gwenda drew a deep breath.

"And you think that's what happened to me? But why don't I remember it all *now*?"

"One can't remember to order. And often when one tries to, the memory goes farther away. But I think there are one or two indications that that is what did happen. For instance when you told me just now about your experience in the theatre last night, you used a very revealing turn of words. You said you seemed to be looking 'through the banisters'—but normally, you know, one doesn't look down into a hall *through* the banisters but *over* them. Only a child would look *through*."

"That's clever of you," said Gwenda appreciatively.

"These little things are very significant."

"But who was Helen?" asked Gwenda in a bewildered way.

"Tell me, my dear, are you still quite sure it was Helen?"

"Yes. . . . It's frightfully odd, because I

don't know who 'Helen' is—but at the same time I do know—I mean I know that it was 'Helen' lying there. . . . How am I going to find out more?"

"Well, I think the obvious thing to do is to find out definitely if you ever were in England as a child, or if you could have been. Your relations—"

Gwenda interrupted. "Aunt Alison. She would know, I'm sure."

"Then I should write to her by airmail. Or send a night mail letter. Tell her circumstances have arisen which make it imperative for you to know if you have ever been in England. You would probably get an answer by airmail by the time your husband arrives."

"Oh, thank you, Miss Marple. You've been frightfully kind. And I do hope what you've suggested is true. Because if so, well, it's quite all right. I mean, it won't be anything supernatural."

Miss Marple smiled.

"I hope it turns out as we think. I am going to stay with some old friends of mine in the North of England the day after tomorrow. I shall be passing back through London in about ten days. If you and your husband are here then, or if you have received an answer to your letter, I should be very curious to know the result."

"Of course, dear Miss Marple! Anyway, I want you to meet Giles. He's a perfect pet.

And we'll have a good powwow about the whole thing."

Gwenda's spirits were fully restored by now.

Miss Marple, however, looked thoughtful.

5

Murder in Retrospect

It was some ten days later that Miss Marple entered a small hotel in Mayfair, and was given an enthusiastic reception by young Mr. and Mrs. Reed.

"This is my husband, Miss Marple. Giles, I can't tell you how kind Miss Marple was to me."

"I'm delighted to meet you, Miss Marple. I hear Gwenda nearly panicked herself into a lunatic asylum."

Miss Marple's gentle blue eyes summed up Giles Reed favourably. A very likeable young man, tall and fair, with a disarming way of blinking every now and then out of a natural shyness. She noted his determined chin and the set of his jaw.

"We'll have tea in the little writing room, the dark one," said Gwenda. "Nobody ever comes there. And then we can show Miss Marple Aunt Alison's letter.

43

"Yes," she added, as Miss Marple looked up sharply. "It's come, and it's almost exactly what you thought."

Tea over, the airmail letter was spread out and read.

Dearest Gwenda, [Miss Danby had written]
I was much disturbed to hear that you had had some worrying experience. To tell you the truth, it had really entirely escaped my memory that you had actually resided for a short time in England as a young child.

Your mother, my sister Megan, met your father, Major Halliday, when she was on a visit to some friends of ours at that time stationed in India. They were married and you were born there. About two years after your birth your mother died. It was a great shock to us and we wrote to your father, with whom we had corresponded, but whom actually we had never seen, begging him to entrust you to our care, as we would be only too glad to have you, and it might be difficult for an Army man stranded with a young child. Your father, however, refused, and told us he was resigning from the Army and taking you back with him to England. He said he hoped we would at some time come over and visit him there.

I understand that on the voyage home, your father met a young woman, became engaged to her, and married her as soon as he got to England. The marriage was not, I gather, a happy one, and I understand they parted about a year later. It was then that your father wrote to us and asked if we were still willing to give you a home. I need hardly tell you, my dear, how happy we were to do so. You were sent out to us in charge of an English nurse, and at the same time your father settled the bulk of his estate upon you and suggested that you might legally adopt our name. This, I may say, seemed a little curious to us, but we felt that it was kindly meant—and intended to make you more one of the family —we did not, however, adopt that suggestion. About a year later your father died in a nursing home. I surmise that he had already received bad news about his health at the time when he sent you out to us.

I'm afraid I cannot tell you where you lived while with your father in England. His letter naturally had the address on it at the time, but that is now eighteen years ago and I'm afraid one doesn't remember such details. It was in the South of England, I know—and I fancy Dillmouth is correct. I had a vague idea it was Dartmouth, but the two names are not unlike. I believe your stepmother married again, but I have no recollection of her name, not even of her unmarried name, though your father had mentioned it in the original letter telling of his remarriage. We were, I think, a little resentful of his marrying again so soon, but of course one knows that on board ship the influence of propinquity is very great—and he may also have thought that it would be a good thing on your account.

It seems stupid of me not to have mentioned to you that you had been in England even if you didn't remember the fact, but, as I say, the whole thing had faded from my mind. Your mother's death in India and your subsequently coming to live with us always seemed the important points.

I hope this is all cleared up now?

I do trust Giles will soon be able to join you. It is hard for you both being parted at this early stage.

All my news in my next letter, as I am sending this off hurriedly in answer to your wire.

> Your loving aunt,
> *Alison Danby*

P.S. You do not say what your worrying experience was?

"You see," said Gwenda. "It's almost exactly as you suggested."

Miss Marple smoothed out the flimsy sheet.

"Yes—yes, indeed. The common-sense explanation. I've found, you know, that that is so often right."

"Well, I'm very grateful to you, Miss Marple," said Giles. "Poor Gwenda was thoroughly upset, and I must say I'd have been rather worried myself to think that Gwenda was clairvoyant or psychic or something."

"It might be a disturbing quality in a wife," said Gwenda. "Unless you've always led a thoroughly blameless life."

"Which I have," said Giles.

"And the house? What do you feel about the house?" asked Miss Marple.

"Oh, that's all right. We're going down tomorrow. Giles is dying to see it."

"I don't know whether you realize it, Miss Marple," said Giles, "but what it amounts to is that we've got a first-class murder mystery on our hands. Actually on our very doorstep —or more accurately in our front hall."

"I *had* thought of that, yes," said Miss Marple slowly.

"And Giles simply loves detective stories," said Gwenda.

"Well, I mean, it *is* a detective story. Body in the hall of a beautiful strangled woman. Nothing known of her but her Christian name. Of course I know it's nearly twenty years ago. There can't be any clues after all this time, but one can at least cast about, and try to pick up some of the threads. Oh! I daresay one won't succeed in solving the riddle—"

"I think you might," said Miss Marple. "Even after eighteen years. Yes, I think you might."

"But at any rate it won't do any harm to have a real good try?"

Giles paused, his face beaming.

Miss Marple moved uneasily, her face was grave—almost troubled.

"But it might do a great deal of harm," she said. "I would advise you both—oh yes, I really would advise it very strongly—to leave the whole thing alone."

"Leave it alone? Our very own murder mystery—if it *was* murder?"

"It was murder, I think. And that's just why I should leave it alone. Murder isn't—it really isn't—a thing to tamper with light-heartedly."

Giles said:

"But, Miss Marple, if everybody felt like that—"

She interrupted him.

"Oh, I know. There are times when it is one's *duty*—an innocent person accused—suspicion resting on various other people—a dangerous criminal at large who may strike again. But you must realize that this murder is very much in the *past*. Presumably it wasn't known for murder. If so, you would have heard fast enough from your old gardener or someone down there. A murder, however long ago, is always news. No, the body must have been disposed of somehow, and the whole thing never suspected. Are you sure—are you really sure—that you are wise to dig it all up again?"

"Miss Marple," cried Gwenda, "you sound really concerned?"

"I am, my dear. You are two very nice and charming young people (if you will allow me to say so). You are newly married and happy together. Don't, I beg of you, start to uncover things that may—well, that may—

how shall I put it?—that may *upset* and *distress* you."

Gwenda stared at her. "You're thinking of something special—of something— What is it you're hinting at?"

"Not hinting, dear. Just advising you (because I've lived a long time and know how very upsetting human nature can be) to let well alone. That's *my* advice, *let well alone.*"

"But it isn't letting well alone." Giles's voice held a different note, a sterner note. "Hillside is our house, Gwenda's and mine, and someone was murdered in that house, or so we believe. I'm not going to stand for murder in my house and do nothing about it, even if it *is* eighteen years ago!"

Miss Marple sighed. "I'm sorry," she said. "I imagine that most young men of spirit would feel like that. I even sympathize and almost admire you for it. But I wish—oh, I do wish—that you wouldn't do it."

II

On the following day, news went round the village of St. Mary Mead that Miss Marple was at home again. She was seen in the High Street at eleven o'clock. She called at the vicarage at ten minutes to twelve. That afternoon three of the gossipy ladies of the village called upon her and obtained her impressions of the gay Metropolis and, this tribute to politeness over, themselves plunged into details of an approaching battle over the fancywork stall at the fete and the position of the tea tent.

Later that evening Miss Marple could be seen as usual in her garden, but for once her activities were more concentrated on the depredations of weeds than on the activities of her neighbours. She was *distraite* at her frugal evening meal, and hardly appeared to listen to her little maid Evelyn's spirited account of the goings-on of the local chemist. The next day she was still *distraite*, and one or two people, including the vicar's wife, remarked upon it. That evening Miss Marple said that she did not feel very well and took to her bed. The following morning she sent for Dr. Haydock.

Dr. Haydock had been Miss Marple's physician, friend and ally for many years. He listened to her account of her symptoms, gave her an examination, then sat back in his chair and waggled his stethoscope at her.

"For a woman of your age," he said, "and in spite of that misleading frail appearance, you're in remarkably good fettle."

"I'm sure my general health is sound," said Miss Marple. "But I confess I do feel a little overtired—a little run-down."

"You've been gallivanting about. Late nights in London."

"That, of course. I do find London a little

tiring nowadays. And the air—so used-up. Not like fresh seaside air."

"The air of St. Mary Mead is nice and fresh."

"But often damp and rather muggy. Not, you know, exactly *bracing*."

Dr. Haydock eyed her with a dawning of interest.

"I'll send you round a tonic," he said obligingly.

"Thank you, Doctor. Easton's syrup is always very helpful."

"There's no need for you to do my prescribing for me, woman."

"I wondered if, perhaps, a change of air—?"

Miss Marple looked questioningly at him with guileless blue eyes.

"You've just been away for three weeks."

"I know. But to London which, as you say, is enervating. And then up North—a manufacturing district. Not like bracing sea air."

Dr. Haydock packed up his bag. Then he turned round, grinning.

"Let's hear why you sent for me," he said. "Just tell me what it's to be and I'll repeat it after you. You want my professional opinion that what you need is sea air—"

"I knew you'd understand," said Miss Marple gratefully.

"Excellent thing, sea air. You'd better go

to Eastbourne right away, or your health may suffer seriously."

"Eastbourne, I think, is rather cold. The downs, you know."

"Bournemouth, then, or the Isle of Wight."

Miss Marple twinkled at him.

"I always think a small place is much pleasanter."

Dr. Haydock sat down again.

"My curiosity is roused. What small seaside town are you suggesting?"

"Well, I *had* thought of Dillmouth."

"Pretty little place. Rather dull. Why Dillmouth?"

For a moment or two Miss Marple was silent. The worried look had returned to her eyes. She said:

"Supposing that one day, by accident, you turned up a fact that seemed to indicate that many years ago—nineteen or twenty—a murder had occurred. That fact was known to you alone, nothing of the kind had ever been suspected or reported. What would you do about it?"

"Murder in retrospect, in fact?"

"Just exactly that."

Haydock reflected for a moment.

"There had been no miscarriage of justice? Nobody had suffered as a result of this crime?"

"As far as one can see, no."

"Hm. Murder in retrospect. Sleeping murder. Well, I'll tell you. I'd let sleeping murder lie—that's what I'd do. Messing about with murder is dangerous. It could be *very* dangerous."

"That's what I'm afraid of."

"People say a murderer always repeats his crimes. That's not true. There's a type who commits a crime, manages to get away with it, and is darned careful never to stick a neck out again. I won't say they live happily ever after—I don't believe that's true—there are many kinds of retribution. But outwardly at least all goes well. Perhaps that was so in the case of Madeleine Smith or again in the case of Lizzie Borden. It was nonproven in the case of Madeleine Smith, and Lizzie was acquitted—but many people believe both of those women were guilty. I could name you others. They never repeated their crimes— one crime gave them what they wanted and they were content. But suppose some danger had menaced them? I take it your killer, whoever he or she is, was one of that kind. He committed a crime and got away with it and nobody suspected. But supposing somebody goes poking about, digging into things, turning up stones and exploring avenues and finally, perhaps, hitting the target? What's your killer going to do about it? Just stay there smiling while the hunt comes nearer and nearer? No, if there's no principle involved, I'd say let it alone." He repeated his former phrase: "Let sleeping murder lie."

He added firmly:

"And those are my orders to *you. Let the whole thing alone.*"

"But it's not I who am involved. It's two very delightful children. Let me tell you!"

She told him the story and Haydock listened.

"Extraordinary," he said when she had finished. "Extraordinary coincidence. Extraordinary business altogether. I suppose you see what the implications are?"

"Oh, of course. But I don't think it's occurred to *them* yet."

"It will mean a good deal of unhappiness and they'll wish they'd never meddled with the thing. Skeletons should be kept in their cupboards. Still, you know, I can quite see young Giles's point of view. Dash it all, I couldn't leave the thing alone myself. Even now, I'm curious. . . ."

He broke off and directed a stern glance at Miss Marple.

"So that's what you're doing with your excuses to get to Dillmouth. Mixing yourself up in something that's no concern of yours."

"Not at all, Dr. Haydock. But I'm worried about those two. They're very young and inexperienced and much too trusting and credulous. I feel I ought to be there to look after them."

"So that's why you're going. To look after them! Can't you *ever* leave murder alone, woman? Even murder in retrospect?"

Miss Marple gave a small prim smile.

"But you do think, don't you, that a few weeks at Dillmouth would be beneficial to my health?"

"More likely to be the end of you," said Dr. Haydock. "But you won't listen to me!"

III

On her way to call upon her friends, Colonel and Mrs. Bantry, Miss Marple met Colonel Bantry coming along the drive, his gun in his hand and his spaniel at his heels. He welcomed her cordially.

"Glad to see you back again. How's London?"

Miss Marple said that London was very well. Her nephew had taken her to several plays.

"Highbrow ones, I bet. Only care for a musical comedy myself."

Miss Marple said that she had been to a Russian play that was very interesting, though perhaps a little too long.

"Russians!" said Colonel Bantry explosively. He had once been given a novel by Dostoevski to read in a nursing home.

He added that Miss Marple would find Dolly in the garden.

Mrs. Bantry was almost always to be found in the garden. Gardening was her passion. Her favourite literature was bulb catalogues and her conversation dealt with primulas, bulbs, flowering shrubs and alpine novelties. Miss Marple's first view of her was a substantial posterior clad in faded tweed.

At the sound of approaching steps, Mrs. Bantry reassumed an erect position with a few creaks and winces, her hobby had made her rheumaticky, wiped her hot brow with an earth-stained hand and welcomed her friend.

"Heard you were back, Jane," she said. "Aren't my new delphiniums doing well? Have you seen these new little gentians? I've had a bit of trouble with them, but I think they're all set now. What we need is rain. It's been terribly dry." She added, "Esther told me you were ill in bed." Esther was Mrs. Bantry's cook and liaison officer with the village. "I'm glad to see it's not true."

"Just a little overtired," said Miss Marple. "Dr. Haydock thinks I need some sea air. I'm rather run-down."

"Oh, but you couldn't go away *now*," said Mrs. Bantry. "This is absolutely the best time of the year in the garden. Your border must be just coming into flower."

"Dr. Haydock thinks it would be advisable."

"Well, Haydock's not such a fool as some doctors," admitted Mrs. Bantry grudgingly.

"I was wondering, Dolly, about that cook of yours."

"Which cook? Do you want a cook? You don't mean that woman who drank, do you?"

"No, no, no. I mean the one who made such delicious pastry. With a husband who was the butler."

"Oh, you mean the Mock Turtle," said Mrs. Bantry with immediate recognition. "Woman with a deep mournful voice who always sounded as though she was just going to burst into tears. She *was* a good cook. Husband was a fat, rather lazy man. Arthur always said he watered the whisky. I don't know. Pity there's always one of a couple that's unsatisfactory. They got left a legacy by some former employer and they went off and opened a boarding house on the South coast."

"That's just what I thought. Wasn't it at Dillmouth?"

"That's right. Fourteen Sea Parade, Dillmouth."

"I was thinking that as Dr. Haydock has suggested the seaside, I might go to—was their name Saunders?"

"Yes. That's an excellent idea, Jane. You couldn't do better. Mrs. Saunders will look after you well, and as it's out of the season, they'll be glad to get you and won't charge very much. With good cooking and sea air you'll soon pick up."

"Thank you, Dolly," said Miss Marple, "I expect I shall."

6

Exercise in Detection

"Where do you think the body was? About here?" asked Giles.

He and Gwenda were standing in the front hall of Hillside. They had arrived back the night before, and Giles was now in full cry. He was as pleased as a small boy with his new toy.

"Just about," said Gwenda. She retreated up the stairs and peered down critically. "Yes—I think that's about it."

"Crouch down," said Giles. "You're only about three years old, you know."

Gwenda crouched obligingly.

"You couldn't actually see the man who said the words?"

"I can't remember seeing him. He must have been just a bit farther back—yes, there. I could only see his paws."

"*Paws*." Giles frowned.

"They *were* paws. Grey paws—not human."

"But look here, Gwenda. This isn't a kind of Murder in the Rue Morgue. A man doesn't have paws."

"Well, *he* had paws."

Giles looked doubtfully at her.

"You must have imagined that bit afterwards."

Gwenda said slowly:

"Don't you think I may have imagined the whole thing? You know, Giles, I've been thinking. It seems to me far more probable that the whole thing was a *dream*. It might have been. It was the sort of dream a child might have, and be terribly frightened, and go on remembering about. Don't you think really that's the proper explanation? Because nobody in Dillmouth seems to have the faintest idea that there was ever a murder, or a sudden death, or a disappearance or *anything* odd about this house."

Giles looked like a different kind of little boy—a little boy who has had his nice new toy taken away from him.

"I suppose it might have been a nightmare," he admitted grudgingly. Then his face cleared suddenly.

"No," he said. "I don't believe it. You could have dreamt about monkeys' paws and someone dead—but I'm damned if you could have dreamt that quotation from *The Duchess of Malfi*."

"I could have heard someone say it and then dreamt about it afterwards."

"I don't think any child could do that. Not unless you heard it in conditions of great stress—and if that was the case we're back again where we were—hold on, I've got it. It was the *paws* you dreamt. You saw the body and heard the words and you were scared stiff and then you had a nightmare about it, and there were waving monkeys' paws too—probably you were frightened of monkeys."

Gwenda looked slightly dubious—she said slowly:

"I suppose that *might* be it. . . ."

"I wish you could remember a bit more. . . . Come down here in the hall. Shut your eyes. Think . . . Doesn't anything more come back to you?"

"No, it doesn't, Giles. . . . The more I think, the further it all goes away. . . . I mean I'm beginning to doubt now if I ever really saw anything at all. Perhaps the other night I just had a brainstorm in the theatre."

"No. There *was* something. Miss Marple thinks so, too. What about 'Helen'? Surely you must remember something about Helen?"

"I don't remember anything at all. It's just a name."

"It mightn't even be the right name."

"Yes, it was. It *was* Helen."

Gwenda looked obstinate and convinced.

"Then if you're so sure it was Helen, you must know something about her," said Giles reasonably. "Did you know her well? Was she living here? Or just staying here?"

"I tell you I don't *know*." Gwenda was beginning to look strained and nervy.

Giles tried another tack.

"Who else can you remember? Your father?"

"No. I mean, I can't tell. There was always his photograph, you see. Aunt Alison used to say: 'That's your Daddy.' I don't remember him *here*, in this house. . . ."

"And no servants—nurses—anything like that?"

"No-no. The more I try and remember, the more it's all a blank. The things I know are all underneath—like walking to that door automatically. I didn't *remember* a door there. Perhaps if you wouldn't worry me so much, Giles, things would come back more. Anyway, trying to find out about it all is hopeless. It's so long ago."

"Of course it's not hopeless—even old Miss Marple admitted that."

"She didn't help us with any ideas of how to set about it," said Gwenda. "And yet I feel, from the glint in her eye, that she had a few. I wonder how *she* would have gone about it."

"I don't suppose she would be likely to think of ways that we wouldn't," said Giles positively. "We must stop speculating, Gwenda, and set about things in a systematic way. We've made a beginning—I've looked through the parish registers of deaths. There's no 'Helen' of the right age among them. In fact there doesn't seem to be a Helen at all in the period I covered. Ellen Pugg, ninety-four, was the nearest. Now we must think of the next profitable approach. If your father, and presumably your stepmother, lived in this house, they must either have bought it or rented it."

"According to Foster, the gardener, some people called Elworthy had it before the Hengraves and before them Mrs. Findeyson. Nobody else."

"Your father might have bought it and lived in it for a very short time—and then sold it again. But I think that it's much more likely that he rented it—probably rented it furnished. If so, our best bet is to go round the house agents."

Going round the house agents was not a prolonged labour. There were only two house agents in Dillmouth. Messrs. Wilkinson were a comparatively new arrival. They had only opened their premises eleven years ago. They dealt mostly with the small bungalows and new houses at the far end of the town. The other agents, Messrs. Galbraith and Penderley, were the ones from whom Gwenda had bought the house. Calling upon them, Giles plunged into his story. He and his wife were delighted with Hillside and with Dillmouth generally. Mrs. Reed had only just discovered that she had actually lived in Dillmouth as a small child. She had some very faint memories of the place, and had an idea that Hillside was actually the house in which she had lived but could not be quite certain about it. Had they any record of the house being let to a Major Halliday? It would be about eighteen or nineteen years ago. . . .

Mr. Penderley stretched out apologetic hands.

"I'm afraid it's not possible to tell you, Mr. Reed. Our records do not go back that far—not, that is, of furnished or short-period lets. Very sorry I can't help you, Mr. Reed. As a matter of fact, if our old head clerk, Mr. Narracott, had still been alive—he died last winter—he might have been able to assist you. A most remarkable memory, really quite remarkable. He had been with the firm for nearly thirty years."

"There's no one else who would possibly remember?"

"Our staff is all on the comparatively young side. Of course there is old Mr. Galbraith himself. He retired some years ago."

"Perhaps I could ask him?" said Gwenda.

"Well, I hardly know about that. . . ." Mr. Penderley was dubious. "He had a stroke last year. His faculties are sadly impaired. He's over eighty, you know."

"Does he live in Dillmouth?"

"Oh yes. At Calcutta Lodge. A very nice little property on the Seaton road. But I really don't think—"

II

"It's rather a forlorn hope," said Giles to Gwenda. "But you never know. I don't think we'll write. We'll go there together and exert our personality."

Calcutta Lodge was surrounded by a neat trim garden, and the sitting room into which they were shown was also neat if slightly overcrowded. It smelt of beeswax and Ronuk. Its brasses shone. Its windows were heavily festooned.

A thin middle-aged woman with suspicious eyes came into the room.

Giles explained himself quickly, and the expression of one who expects to have a vacuum cleaner pushed at her left Miss Galbraith's face.

"I'm sorry, but I really don't think I can help you," she said. "It's so long ago, isn't it?"

"One does sometimes remember things," said Gwenda.

"Of course I shouldn't know anything myself. I never had any connection with the business. A Major Halliday, you said? No, I never remember coming across anyone in Dillmouth of that name."

"Your father might remember, perhaps," said Gwenda.

"Father?" Miss Galbraith shook her head. "He doesn't take much notice nowadays, and his memory's very shaky."

Gwenda's eyes were resting thoughtfully on a Benares brass table and they shifted to a procession of ebony elephants marching along the mantelpiece.

"I thought he might remember, perhaps," she said, "because my father had just come from India. Your house is called Calcutta Lodge?"

She paused interrogatively.

"Yes," said Miss Galbraith. "Father was out in Calcutta for a time. In business there. Then the war came and in nineteen twenty he came into the firm here, but would have liked to go back, he always says. But my mother didn't fancy foreign parts—and of course you can't say the climate's really healthy. Well, I don't know—perhaps you'd like to see my father. I don't know that it's one of his good days—"

She led them into a small back study. Here, propped up in a big shabby leather chair, sat an old gentleman with a white walrus moustache. His face was pulled slightly sideways. He eyed Gwenda with distinct approval as his daughter made the introductions.

"Memory's not what it used to be," he said

in a rather indistinct voice. "Halliday, you say? No, I don't remember the name. Knew a boy at school in Yorkshire—but that's seventy-odd years ago."

"He rented Hillside, we think," said Giles.

"Hillside? Was it called Hillside then?" Mr. Galbraith's one movable eyelid snapped shut and open. "Findeyson lived there. Fine woman."

"My father might have rented it furnished. . . . He'd just come from India."

"India? India, d'you say? Remember a fellow—Army man. Knew that old rascal Mohammed Hassan who cheated me over some carpets. Had a young wife—and a baby —little girl."

"That was me," said Gwenda firmly.

"In-deed—you don't say so! Well, well, time flies. Now what *was* his name? Wanted a place furnished—yes— Mrs. Findeyson had been ordered to Egypt or some such place for the winter—all tomfoolery. Now what was his name?"

"Halliday," said Gwenda.

"That's right, my dear—Halliday. Major Halliday. Nice fellow. Very pretty wife— quite young—fair-haired, wanted to be near her people or something like that. Yes, very pretty."

"Who were her people?"

"No idea at all. No idea. You don't look like her."

Gwenda nearly said: "She was only my stepmother," but refrained from complicating the issue. She said: "What did she look like?"

Unexpectedly Mr. Galbraith replied:

"Looked worried. That's what she looked —worried. Yes, very nice fellow, that Major chap. Interested to hear I'd been out in Calcutta. Not like these chaps that have never been out of England. Narrow—that's what they are. Now *I've* seen the world. What was his name, that Army chap—wanted a furnished house?"

He was like a very old gramophone, repeating a worn record.

"St. Catherine's. That's it. Took St. Catherine's—six guineas a week—while Mrs. Findeyson was in Egypt. Died there, poor soul. House was put up for auction—who bought it now? Elworthys—that's it—pack of women—sisters. Changed the name—said St. Catherine's was popish. Very down on anything popish. Used to send out tracts. Plain women, all of 'em— Took an interest in the natives— Sent 'em out trousers and Bibles. Very strong on converting the heathen."

He sighed suddenly and leant back.

"Long time ago," he said fretfully. "Can't remember names. Chap from India—nice chap. . . . I'm tired, Gladys. I'd like my tea."

Giles and Gwenda thanked him, thanked his daughter, and came away.

"So that's proved," said Gwenda. "My father and I were at Hillside. What do we do next?"

"I've been an idiot," said Giles. "Somerset House."

"What's Somerset House?" asked Gwenda.

"It's a record office where you can look up marriages. I'm going there to look up your father's marriage. According to your aunt, your father was married to his second wife immediately on arriving in England. Don't you see, Gwenda—it ought to have occurred to us before—it's perfectly possible that 'Helen' may have been a relation of your step-mother's—a young sister, perhaps. Anyway, once we know what her surname was, we may be able to get on to someone who knows about the general setup at Hillside. Remember the old boy said they wanted a house in Dillmouth to be near Mrs. Halliday's people. If her people live near here, we may get something."

"Giles," said Gwenda. "I think you're wonderful."

III

Giles did not, after all, find it necessary to go to London. Though his energetic nature always made him prone to rush hither and thither and try to do everything himself, he admitted that a purely routine inquiry could be delegated.

He put through a trunk call to his office.

"Got it," he exclaimed enthusiastically, when the expected reply arrived.

From the covering letter he extracted a certified copy of a marriage certificate.

"Here we are, Gwenda. Friday, August seventh, Kensington Registry Office. Kelvin James Halliday to Helen Spenlove Kennedy."

Gwenda cried out sharply:

"Helen?"

They looked at each other.

Giles said slowly:

"But—but—it can't be *her*. I mean—they separated, and she married again—and went away."

"We don't know," said Gwenda, "that she went away . . ."

She looked again at the plainly written name: *Helen Spenlove Kennedy.*

Helen . . .

7

Dr. Kennedy

A few days later Gwenda, walking along the esplanade in a sharp wind, stopped suddenly beside one of the glass shelters which a thoughtful corporation had provided for the use of its visitors.

"Miss Marple?" she exclaimed in lively surprise.

For indeed Miss Marple it was, nicely wrapped up in a thick fleecy coat and well wound round with scarves.

"Quite a surprise to you, I'm sure, to find me here," said Miss Marple briskly. "But my doctor ordered me away to the seaside for a little change, and your description of Dillmouth sounded so attractive that I decided to come here—especially as the cook and butler of a friend of mine take in boarders."

"But why didn't you come and see us?" demanded Gwenda.

"Old people can be rather a nuisance, my

dear. Newly married young couples should be left to themselves." She smiled at Gwenda's protest. "I'm sure you'd have made me very welcome. And how are you both? And are you progressing with your mystery?"

"We're hot on the trail," Gwenda said, sitting beside her.

She detailed their various investigations up to date.

"And now," she ended, "we've put an advertisement in lots of papers—local ones and the *Times* and the other big dailies. We've just said will anyone with any knowledge of Helen Spenlove Halliday, née Kennedy, communicate, et cetera. I should think, don't you, that we're bound to get *some* answers?"

"I should think so, my dear—yes, I should think so."

Miss Marple's tone was placid as ever, but her eyes looked troubled. They flashed a quick appraising glance at the girl sitting beside her. That tone of determined heartiness did not ring quite true. Gwenda, Miss Marple thought, looked worried. What Dr. Haydock had called "the implications" were, perhaps, beginning to occur to her. Yes, but now it was too late to go back. . . .

Miss Marple said gently and apologetically:

"I have really become most interested in all this. My life, you know, has so *few* excitements. I hope you won't think me *very* inquisitive if I ask you to let me know how you progress?"

"Of course we'll let you know," said Gwenda warmly. "You shall be in on everything. Why, but for you, I should be urging doctors to shut me up in a loony bin. Tell me your address here, and then you must come and have a drink—I mean, have tea with us, and see the house. You've got to see the scene of the crime, haven't you?"

She laughed, but there was a slightly nervy edge to her laugh.

When she had gone on her way, Miss Marple shook her head very gently and frowned.

II

Giles and Gwenda scanned the mail eagerly every day, but at first their hopes were disappointed. All they got was two letters from private inquiry agents who pronounced themselves willing and skilled to undertake investigations on their behalf.

"Time enough for them later," said Giles. "And if we do have to employ some agency, it will be a thoroughly first-class firm, not one that touts through the mail. But I don't really see what they could do that we aren't doing."

His optimism (or self-esteem) was justified a few days later. A letter arrived, written in one of those clear and yet somewhat illegible handwritings that stamp the professional man.

> Galls Hill
> Woodleigh Bolton.
> Dear Sir,
>   In answer to your advertisement in the *Times*, Helen Spenlove Kennedy is my sister. I have lost touch with her for many years and should be glad to have news of her.
>
>   Yours faithfully,
>   *James Kennedy*, M.D.

"Woodleigh Bolton," said Giles. "That's not too far away. Woodleigh Camp is where they go for picnics. Up on the moorland. About thirty miles from here. We'll write and ask Dr. Kennedy if we may come and see him, or if he would prefer to come to us."

A reply was received that Dr. Kennedy would be prepared to receive them on the following Wednesday; and on that day they set off.

Woodleigh Bolton was a straggling village set along the side of a hill. Galls Hill was the highest house at the top of the rise, with a view over Woodleigh Camp and the moors towards the sea.

"Rather a bleak spot," said Gwenda, shivering.

The house itself was bleak and obviously Dr. Kennedy scorned such modern innovations as central heating. The woman who opened the door was dark and rather forbidding. She led them across the rather bare hall and into a study where Dr. Kennedy rose to receive them. It was a long, rather high room, lined with well-filled bookshelves.

Dr. Kennedy was a grey-haired elderly man with shrewd eyes under tufted brows. His gaze went sharply from one to the other of them.

"Mr. and Mrs. Reed? Sit here, Mrs. Reed. It's probably the most comfortable chair. Now, what's all this about?"

Giles went fluently into their prearranged story.

He and his wife had been recently married in New Zealand. They had come to England, where his wife had lived for a short time as a child, and she was trying to trace old family friends and connections.

Dr. Kennedy remained stiff and unbending. He was polite but obviously irritated by colonial insistence on sentimental family ties.

"And you think my sister—my half-sister —and possibly myself—are connections of yours?" he asked Gwenda civilly, but with slight hostility.

"She was my stepmother," said Gwenda. "My father's second wife. I can't really remember her properly, of course. I was so small. My maiden name was Halliday."

He stared at her—and then suddenly a smile illuminated his face. He became a different person, no longer aloof.

"Good Lord," he said. "Don't tell me that you're Gwennie!"

Gwenda nodded eagerly. The pet name, long forgotten, sounded in her ears with reassuring familiarity.

"Yes," she said. "I'm Gwennie."

"God bless my soul. Grown-up and married. How times flies! It must be—what—fifteen years—no, of course, much longer than that. You don't remember me, I suppose?"

Gwenda shook her head.

"I don't even remember my father. I mean it's all a vague kind of blur."

"Of course—Halliday's first wife came from New Zealand—I remember his telling me so. A fine country, I should think."

"It's the loveliest country in the world—but I'm quite fond of England, too."

"On a visit—or settling down here?" He rang the bell. "We must have tea."

When the tall woman came, he said, "Tea, please—and—er—hot buttered toast, or—or cake, or something."

The respectable housekeeper looked venomous, but said "Yes, sir," and went out.

"I don't usually go in for tea," said Dr. Kennedy vaguely. "But we must celebrate."

"It's very nice of you," said Gwenda. "No, we're not on a visit. We've bought a house." She paused and added, "Hillside."

Dr. Kennedy said vaguely:

"Oh yes. In Dillmouth. You wrote from there."

"It's the most extraordinary coincidence," said Gwenda. "Isn't it, Giles?"

"I should say so," said Giles. "Really quite staggering."

"It was for sale, you see," said Gwenda, and added in face of Dr. Kennedy's apparent noncomprehension, "It's the same house where we used to live long ago."

Dr. Kennedy frowned. "Hillside? But surely— Oh yes, I did hear they'd changed the name. Used to be St. something or other —if I'm thinking of the right house—on the Leahampton road, coming down into the town, on the right-hand side?"

"Yes."

"That's the one. Funny how names go out of your head. Wait a minute. St. Catherine's —that's what it used to be called."

"And I did live there, didn't I?" Gwenda said.

"Yes, of course you did." He stared at her, amused. "Why did you want to come back there? You can't remember much about it, surely?"

"No. But somehow—it felt like home."

"It felt like home," the doctor repeated.

There was no expression in the words, but Giles wondered suddenly what he was thinking about.

"So you see," said Gwenda, "I hoped you'd tell me about it all—about my father and Helen and—" she ended lamely—"and everything. . . ."

He looked at her reflectively.

"I suppose they didn't know very much—out in New Zealand. Why should they? Well, there isn't much to tell. Helen—my sister—was coming back from India on the same boat with your father. He was a widower with a small daughter. Helen was sorry for him or fell in love with him. He was lonely, or fell in love with her. Difficult to know just the way things happen. They were married in London on arrival, and came down to Dillmouth to me. I was in practice there then. Kelvin Halliday seemed a nice chap, rather nervy and run-down—but they seemed happy enough together—then."

He was silent for a moment before he said:

"However, in less than a year, she ran away with someone else. You probably know that?"

"Who did she run away with?" asked Gwenda.

He bent his shrewd eyes upon her.

"She didn't tell me," he said, "I wasn't in her confidence. I'd seen—couldn't help seeing—that there was friction between her and Kelvin. I didn't know why. I was always a strait-laced sort of fellow—a believer in marital fidelity. Helen wouldn't have wanted me to know what was going on. I'd heard rumours—one does—but there was no mention of any particular name. They often had guests staying with them who came from London or from other parts of England. I imagined it was one of them."

"There wasn't a divorce, then?"

"Helen didn't want a divorce. Kelvin told me that. That's why I imagined, perhaps wrongly, that it was a case of some married man. Someone whose wife was an R.C. perhaps."

"And my father?"

"He didn't want a divorce either."

Dr. Kennedy spoke rather shortly.

"Tell me about my father," said Gwenda. "Why did he decide suddenly to send me out to New Zealand?"

Kennedy paused a moment before saying:

"I gather your people out there had been pressing him. After the breakup of his second marriage, he probably thought it was the best thing."

"Why didn't he take me out there himself?"

Dr. Kennedy looked along the mantelpiece, searching vaguely for a pipe cleaner.

"Oh, I don't know. . . . He was in rather poor health."

"What was the matter with him? What did he die of?"

The door opened and the scornful house-keeper appeared with a laden tray.

There was buttered toast and some jam, but no cake. With a vague gesture Dr. Kennedy motioned Gwenda to pour out. She did so. When the cups were filled and handed round and Gwenda had taken a piece of toast, Dr. Kennedy said with rather forced cheerfulness:

"Tell me what you've done to the house? Made a lot of changes and improvements? I don't suppose I'd recognize it now—after you two have finished with it."

"We're having a little fun with bathrooms," admitted Giles.

Gwenda, her eyes on the doctor, said:

"What did my father die of?"

"I couldn't really tell you, my dear. As I say, he was in rather poor health for a while, and he finally went into a sanatorium—somewhere on the East coast. He died about two years later."

"Where was this sanatorium exactly?"

"I'm sorry. I can't remember now. As I say, I have an impression it was on the East coast."

There was definite evasion now in his manner. Giles and Gwenda looked at each other for a brief second.

Giles said:

"At least, sir, you can tell us where he's buried? Gwenda is—naturally—very anxious to visit his grave."

Dr. Kennedy bent over the fireplace, scraping in the bowl of his pipe with a penknife.

"Do you know," he said rather indistinctly, "I don't really think I should dwell too much on the past. All this ancestor worship—it's a mistake. The future is what matters. Here you are, you two, young and healthy, with the world in front of you. Think forward. No use going about putting flowers on the grave of someone whom, for all practical purposes, you hardly knew."

Gwenda said mutinously:

"I should like to see my father's grave."

"I'm afraid I can't help you." Dr. Kennedy's tones were pleasant but cold. "It's a long time ago, and my memory isn't what it was. I lost touch with your father after he left Dillmouth. I think he wrote to me once from the sanatorium and, as I say, I have an impression it was on the East coast—but I couldn't really be sure even of that. And I've no idea at all of where he is buried."

"How very odd," said Giles.

"Not really. The link between us, you see, was Helen. I was always very fond of Helen. She's my half-sister and very many years younger than I am, but I tried to bring her up as well as I could. The right schools and all that. But there's no gainsaying that Helen

—well, that she never had a stable character. There was trouble when she was quite young with a very undesirable young man. I got her out of that safely. Then she elected to go out to India and marry Walter Fane. Well, that was all right, nice lad, son of Dillmouth's leading solicitor, but frankly, dull as ditchwater. He'd always adored her, but she never looked at him. Still, she changed her mind and went out to India to marry him. When she saw him again, it was all off. She wired to me for money for her passage home. I sent it. On the way back, she met Kelvin. They were married before I knew about it. I've felt, shall we say, apologetic for that sister of mine. It explains why Kelvin and I didn't keep up the relationship after she went away." He added suddenly: "Where's Helen now? Can you tell me? I'd like to get in touch with her."

"But we don't know," said Gwenda. "We don't know at all."

"Oh! I thought from your advertisement—" He looked at them with sudden curiosity. "Tell me, why did you advertise?"

Gwenda said:

"We wanted to get in touch—" and stopped.

"With someone you can hardly remember?" Dr. Kennedy looked puzzled.

Gwenda said quickly:

"I thought—if I could get in touch with her—she'd tell me—about my father."

"Yes—yes—I see. Sorry I can't be of much use. Memory not what it was. And it's a long time ago."

"At least," said Giles, "you know what kind of a sanatorium it was? Tubercular?"

Dr. Kennedy's face again looked suddenly wooden.

"Yes—yes, I rather believe it was."

"Then we ought to be able to trace that quite easily," said Giles. "Thank you very much, sir, for all you've told us."

He got up and Gwenda followed suit.

"Thank you very much," she said. "And do come and see us at Hillside."

They went out of the room and Gwenda, glancing back over her shoulder, had a final view of Dr. Kennedy standing by the mantelpiece, pulling his grizzled moustache and looking troubled.

"He knows something he won't tell us," said Gwenda, as they got into the car. "There's *something*—oh, Giles! I wish—I wish now that we'd never started. . . ."

They looked at each other, and in each mind, unacknowledged to the other, the same fear sprang.

"Miss Marple was right," said Gwenda. "We should have left the past alone."

"We needn't go any further," said Giles uncertainly. "I think perhaps, Gwenda darling, we'd better not."

Gwenda shook her head.

"No, Giles, we can't stop now. We should

always be wondering and imagining. No, we've got to go on. . . . Dr. Kennedy wouldn't tell us because he wanted to be kind—but that sort of kindness is no good. We'll have to go on and find out what really happened. Even if—even if—it was my father who . . ."

But she couldn't go on.

8

Kelvin Halliday's Delusion

They were in the garden on the following morning when Mrs. Cocker came out and said:

"Excuse me, sir. There's a Dr. Kennedy on the telephone."

Leaving Gwenda in consultation with old Foster, Giles went into the house and picked up the telephone receiver.

"Giles Reed here."

"This is Dr. Kennedy. I've been thinking over our conversation yesterday, Mr. Reed. There are certain facts which I think perhaps you and your wife ought to know. Will you be at home if I come over this afternoon?"

"Certainly we shall. What time?"

"Three o'clock?"

"Suits us."

In the garden old Foster said to Gwenda:

"Is that Dr. Kennedy as used to live over at West Cliff?"

"I expect so. Did you know him?"

" 'E was allus reckoned to be the best doctor here—not but what Dr. Lazenby wasn't more popular. Always had a word and a laugh to jolly you along, Dr. Lazenby did. Dr. Kennedy was always short and a bit dry-like—but he knew his job."

"When did he give up his practice?"

"Long time ago now. Must be fifteen years or so. His health broke down, so they say."

Giles came out of the window and answered Gwenda's unspoken question.

"He's coming over this afternoon."

"Oh." She turned once more to Foster. "Did you know Dr. Kennedy's sister at all?"

"Sister? Not as I remember. She was only a bit of a lass. Went away to school, and then abroad, though I heard she come back here for a bit after she married. But I believe she run off with some chap—always wild she was, they said. Don't know as I ever laid eyes on her myself. I was in a job over to Plymouth for a while, you know."

Gwenda said to Giles as they walked to the end of the terrace:

"Why is he coming?"

"We'll know at three o'clock."

Dr. Kennedy arrived punctually. Looking round the drawing room, he said: "Seems odd to be here again."

Then he came to the point without preamble.

"I take it that you two are quite determined

to track down the sanatorium where Kelvin Halliday died and learn all the details you can about his illness and death?"

"Definitely," said Gwenda.

"Well, you can manage that quite easily, of course. So I've come to the conclusion that it will be less shock to you to hear the facts from me. I'm sorry to have to tell you, for it won't do you or anybody else a bit of good, and it will probably cause *you*, Gwennie, a good deal of pain. But there it is. Your father wasn't suffering from tuberculosis and the sanatorium in question was a mental home."

"A mental home? Was he out of his mind, then?"

Gwenda's face had gone very white.

"He was never certified. And in my opinion he was not insane in the general meaning of the term. He had had a very severe nervous breakdown and suffered from certain delusional obsessions. He went into the nursing home of his own will and volition and could, of course, have left it at any time he wanted to. His condition did not improve, however, and he died there."

"Delusional obsessions?" Giles repeated the words questioningly. "What kind of delusions?"

Dr. Kennedy said drily:

"He was under the impression that he had strangled his wife."

Gwenda gave a stifled cry. Giles stretched out a hand quickly and took her cold hand in his.

Giles said:

"And—and had he?"

"Eh?" Dr. Kennedy stared at him. "No, of course he hadn't. No question of such a thing."

"But—but how do you know?" Gwenda's voice came uncertainly.

"My dear child! There was never any question of such a thing. Helen left him for another man. He'd been in a very unbalanced condition for some time; nervous dreams, sick fancies. The final shock sent him over the edge. I'm not a psychologist myself. They have their explanations for such matters. If a man would rather his wife was dead than unfaithful, he can manage to make himself believe that she is dead—even that he has killed her."

Warily, Giles and Gwenda exchanged a warning glance.

Giles said quietly:

"So you are quite sure that there was no question of his having actually done what he said he had done?"

"Oh, quite sure. I had two letters from Helen. The first one from France about a week after she went away and one about six months later. Oh no, the whole thing was a delusion pure and simple."

Gwenda drew a deep breath.

"Please," she said. "Will you tell me all about it?"

"I'll tell you everything I can, my dear. To begin with, Kelvin had been in a rather peculiar neurotic state for some time. He came to me about it. Said he had had various disquieting dreams. These dreams, he said, were always the same, and they ended in the same way—with his throttling Helen. I tried to get at the root of the trouble—there must, I think, have been some conflict in early childhood. His father and mother apparently were not a happy couple. . . . Well, I won't go into all that. That's only interesting to a medical man. I actually suggested that Kelvin should consult a psychologist, there are several first-class chaps—but he wouldn't hear of it—thought that kind of thing was all nonsense.

"I had an idea that he and Helen weren't getting along too well, but he never spoke about that, and I didn't like to ask questions. The whole thing came to a head when he walked into my house one evening—it was a Friday, I remember, I'd just come back from the hospital and found him waiting for me in the consulting room; he'd been there about a quarter of an hour. As soon as I came in, he looked up and said:

" '*I've killed Helen.*'

"For a moment I didn't know what to think.

He was so cool and matter-of-fact. I said: 'You mean—you've had another dream?' He said: 'It isn't a dream this time. It's true. She's lying there strangled. I strangled her.'

"Then he said—quite coolly and reasonably: 'You'd better come back with me to the house. Then you can ring up the police from there.' I didn't know what to think. I got out the car again, and we drove along here. The house was quiet and dark. We went up to the bedroom—"

Gwenda broke in: "*The bedroom?*" Her voice held pure astonishment.

Dr. Kennedy looked faintly surprised.

"Yes, yes, that's where it all happened. Well, of course when we got up there—there was nothing at all! No dead woman lying across the bed. Nothing disturbed—the coverlets not even rumpled. The whole thing had been pure hallucination."

"But what did my father say?"

"Oh, he persisted in his story, of course. He really believed it, you see. I persuaded him to let me give him a sedative and I put him to bed in the dressing room. Then I had a good look round. I found a note that Helen had left crumpled up in the waste-paper basket in the drawing room. It was quite clear. She had written something like this: 'This is good-bye. I'm sorry—but our marriage has been a mistake from the beginning. I'm going away with the only man I've ever loved. Forgive me if you can. Helen.'

"Evidently Kelvin had come in, read her note, gone upstairs, had a kind of emotional brainstorm and had then come over to me persuaded that he had killed Helen.

"Then I questioned the housemaid. It was her evening out and she had come in late. I took her into Helen's room and she went through Helen's clothes. It was all quite clear. Helen had packed a suitcase and a bag and had taken them away with her. I searched the house, but there was no trace of anything unusual—certainly no sign of a strangled woman.

"I had a very difficult time with Kelvin in the morning, but he realized at last that it was a delusion—or at least he said he did, and he consented to go into a nursing home for treatment.

"A week later I got, as I say, a letter from Helen. It was posted from Biarritz, but she said she was going on to Spain. I was to tell Kelvin that she did not want a divorce. He had better forget her as soon as possible.

"I showed the letter to Kelvin. He said very little. He was going ahead with his plans. He wired out to his first wife's people in New Zealand, asking them to take the child. He settled up his affairs and he then entered a very good private mental home and consented to have appropriate treatment. That treatment, however, did nothing to help him. He died there two years later. I can give you the address of the place. It's in Norfolk. The present superintendent was a young doctor there at the time, and will probably be able to give you full details of your father's case."

Gwenda said:

"And you got another letter from your sister—after that again?"

"Oh yes. About six months later. She wrote from Florence—gave an address poste restante as 'Miss Kennedy.' She said she realized that perhaps it was unfair to Kelvin not to have a divorce—though she herself did not want one. If he wanted a divorce and I would let her know, she would see that he had the necessary evidence. I took the letter to Kelvin. He said at once that he did not want a divorce. I wrote to her and told her so. Since then I have never heard any more. I don't know where she is living, or indeed if she is alive or dead. That is why I was attracted by your advertisement and hoped that I should get news of her."

He added gently:

"I'm very sorry about this, Gwennie. But you had to know. I only wish you could have left well alone. . . ."

9

Unknown Factor?

When Giles came back from seeing Dr. Kennedy off, he found Gwenda sitting where he had left her. There was a bright red patch on each of her cheeks, and her eyes looked feverish. When she spoke, her voice was harsh and brittle.

"What's the old catch phrase? Death or madness either way? That's what this is— death or madness."

"Gwenda—darling." Giles went to her— put his arm round her. Her body felt hard and stiff.

"Why didn't we leave it all alone? Why didn't we? It was my own father who strangled her. And it was my own father's voice I heard saying those words. No wonder it all came back—no wonder I was so frightened. My own father."

"Wait, Gwenda—wait. We don't really know—"

"Of course we know! He told Dr. Kennedy he had strangled his wife, didn't he?"

"But Kennedy is quite positive he didn't—"

"Because he didn't find a body. But there *was* a body—and I *saw* it."

"You saw it in the hall—not the bedroom."

"What difference does that make?"

"Well, it's queer, isn't it? Why should Halliday say he strangled his wife in the bedroom if he actually strangled her in the hall?"

"Oh, I don't know. That's just a minor detail."

"I'm not so sure. Pull your socks up, darling. There are some very funny points about the whole setup. We'll take it, if you like, that your father *did* strangle Helen. In the hall. What happened next?"

"He went off to Dr. Kennedy."

"And told him he had strangled his wife in the bedroom, brought him back with him and there was no body in the hall—*or* in the bedroom. Dash it all, there can't be a murder without a body. What had he done with the body?"

"Perhaps there was one and Dr. Kennedy helped him and hushed it all up—only of course he couldn't tell *us* that."

Giles shook his head.

"No, Gwenda—I don't see Kennedy acting that way. He's a hardheaded, shrewd unemotional Scotsman. You're suggesting that he'd be willing to put himself in jeopardy as an accessory after the fact. I don't believe he would. He'd do his best for Halliday by giving evidence as to his mental state—that, yes. But why should he stick his neck out to hush the whole thing up? Kelvin Halliday wasn't any relation to him, nor a close friend. It was his own sister who had been killed and he was clearly fond of her—even if he did show slight Victorian disapproval of her gay ways. It's not, even, as though *you* were his sister's child. No, Kennedy wouldn't connive at concealing murder. If he did, there's only one possible way he could have set about it, and that would be deliberately to give a death certificate that she had died of heart failure or something. I suppose he *might* have got away with that—but we know definitely that he didn't do that. Because there's no record of her death in the parish registers, and if he had done it, he would have told us that his sister had died. So go on from there and explain, if you can, what happened to the body."

"Perhaps my father buried it somewhere —in the garden?"

"And *then* went to Kennedy and told him he'd murdered his wife? Why? Why not rely on the story that she'd 'left him?'"

Gwenda pushed back her hair from her forehead. She was less stiff and rigid now, and the patches of sharp colour were fading.

"I don't know," she admitted. "It does seem

a bit screwy now you've put it that way. Do you think Dr. Kennedy was telling us the truth?"

"Oh yes—I'm pretty sure of it. From his point of view it's a perfectly reasonable story. Dreams, hallucinations—finally a major hallucination. He's got no doubt that it was a hallucination because, as we've just said, you can't have a murder without a body. That's where we're in a different position from him. We know that there was a body."

He paused and went on.

"From his point of view, everything fits in. Missing clothes and suitcase, the farewell note. And later, two letters from his sister."

Gwenda stirred.

"Those letters. How do we explain those?"

"We don't—but we've got to. If we assume that Kennedy was telling us the truth (and as I say, I'm pretty sure that he was), we've got to explain those letters."

"I suppose they really were in his sister's handwriting? He recognized it?"

"You know, Gwenda, I don't believe that point would arise. It's not like a signature on a doubtful check. If those letters were written in a reasonably close imitation of his sister's writing, it wouldn't occur to him to doubt them. He's already got the preconceived idea that she's gone away with someone. The letters just confirmed that belief. If he had never heard from her at all—why, then he *might* have got suspicious. All the same, there are certain curious points about those letters that wouldn't strike him, perhaps, but do strike me. They're strangely anonymous. No address except a poste restante. No indication of who the man in the case was. A clearly stated determination to make a clean break with all old ties. What I mean is, they're exactly the kind of letters a *murderer* would devise if he wanted to allay any suspicions on the part of his victim's family. It's the old Crippen touch again. To get the letters posted from abroad would be easy."

"You think my father—"

"*No*—that's just it—I *don't*. Take a man who's deliberately decided to get rid of his wife. He spreads rumours about her possible unfaithfulness. He stages the departure—note left behind, clothes packed and taken. Letters will be received from her at carefully spaced intervals from somewhere abroad. Actually he has murdered her quietly and put her, say, under the cellar floor. That's one pattern of murder—and it's often been done. But what that type of murderer *doesn't* do is to rush to his brother-in-law and say he's murdered his wife and hadn't they better go to the police? On the other hand, if your father was the emotional type of killer, and was terribly in love with his wife and strangled her in a fit of frenzied jealousy— Othello fashion (and that fits in with the words you heard)—he certainly doesn't pack clothes and arrange for letters to come, before he rushes off to broadcast his crime to a man who isn't the type likely to hush it up. It's all wrong, Gwenda. The whole pattern is wrong."

"Then what are you trying to get at, Giles?"

"I don't know. . . . It's just that throughout it all, there seems to be an unknown factor —call him X. Someone who hasn't appeared as yet. But one gets glimpses of his technique."

"X?" said Gwenda wonderingly. Then her eyes darkened. "You're making that up, Giles. To comfort me."

"I swear I'm not. Don't you see yourself that you can't make a satisfactory outline to fit all the facts. We know that Helen Halliday was strangled because you saw—"

He stopped.

"Good Lord. I've been a fool. I see it now. It covers everything. You're right. And Kennedy's right, too. Listen, Gwenda. Helen's preparing to go away with a lover—who that is, we don't know."

"X?"

Giles brushed her interpolation aside impatiently.

"She's written her note to her husband—but at that moment he comes in, reads what she's writing and goes haywire. He crumples up the note, slings it into the wastebasket, and goes for her. She's terrified, rushes out into the hall—he catches up with her, throttles her—she goes limp and he drops her. And then, standing a little way from her, he quotes those words from *The Duchess of Malfi* just as the child upstairs has reached the banisters and is peering down."

"And after that?"

"The point is, *that she isn't dead.* He may have thought she was dead—but she's merely semi-suffocated. Perhaps her lover comes round—after the frantic husband has started for the doctor's house on the other side of the town, or perhaps she regains consciousness by herself. Anyway, as soon as she has come to, she beats it. Beats it quickly. And that explains everything. Kelvin's belief that he has killed her. The disappearance of the clothes; packed and taken away earlier in the day. And the subsequent letters *which are perfectly genuine.* There you are—that explains everything."

Gwenda said slowly:

"It doesn't explain why Kelvin said he had strangled her in the bedroom."

"He was so het-up he couldn't quite remember where it had all happened."

Gwenda said:

"I'd like to believe you. I want to believe. . . . But I go on feeling sure—quite sure —that when I looked down, she was dead— quite dead."

"But how could you possibly tell? A child of barely three."

She looked at him queerly.

"I think one can tell—better then than if one was older. It's like dogs—they know death and throw back their heads and howl. I think children—know death. . . ."

"That's nonsense—that's fantastic."

The ring of the front doorbell interrupted him. He said:

"Who's that, I wonder?"

Gwenda looked dismayed.

"I quite forgot. It's Miss Marple. I asked her to tea today. Don't let's say anything about all this to her."

II

Gwenda was afraid that tea might prove a difficult meal—but Miss Marple fortunately seemed not to notice that her hostess talked a little too fast and too feverishly, and that her gaiety was somewhat forced. Miss Marple herself was gently garrulous—she was enjoying her stay in Dillmouth so much and—wasn't it exciting?—some friends of friends of hers had written to friends of theirs in Dillmouth, and as a result she had received some very pleasant invitations from the local residents.

"One feels so much less of an outsider, if you know what I mean, my dear, if one gets to know some of the people who have been established here for years. For instance, I am going to tea with Mrs. Fane—she is the widow of the senior partner in the best firm of solicitors here. Quite an old-fashioned family firm. Her son is carrying it on now."

The gentle gossiping voice went on. Her landlady was so kind—and made her so comfortable—"and really delicious cooking, she was for some years with my old friend Mrs. Bantry—although she does not come from this part of the world herself—her aunt lived here for many years and she and her husband used to come here for holidays—so she knows a great deal of the local gossip. Do you find your gardener satisfactory, by the way? I hear that he is considered locally as rather a *scrimshanker*—more talk than work."

"Talk and tea is his speciality," said Giles. "He has about five cups of tea a day. But he works splendidly when we are looking."

"Come out and see the garden," said Gwenda.

They showed her the house and the garden, and Miss Marple made the proper comments. If Gwenda had feared her shrewd observation of something amiss, then Gwenda was wrong. For Miss Marple showed no cognizance of anything unusual.

Yet, strangely enough, it was Gwenda who acted in an unpredictable manner. She interrupted Miss Marple in the midst of a little anecdote about a child and a seashell to say breathlessly to Giles:

"I don't care—I'm going to tell her. . . ."

Miss Marple turned her head attentively. Giles started to speak, then stopped. Finally he said: "Well, it's your funeral, Gwenda."

And so Gwenda poured it all out. Their call on Dr. Kennedy and his subsequent call on them and what he had told them.

"That was what you meant in London, wasn't it?" Gwenda asked breathlessly. "You thought, then, that—that my father might be involved?"

Miss Marple said gently:

"It occurred to me as a possibility—yes. 'Helen' might very well be a young step-mother—and in a case of—er—strangling, it is so often a husband who is involved."

Miss Marple spoke as one who observes natural phenomena without surprise or emotion.

"I do see why you urged us to leave it alone," said Gwenda. "Oh, and I wish now we had. But one can't go back."

"No," said Miss Marple, "one can't go back."

"And now you'd better listen to Giles. He's been making objections and suggestions."

"All I say is," said Giles, "that it doesn't fit."

And lucidly, clearly, he went over the points as he had previously outlined them to Gwenda.

Then he particularized his final theory.

"If you'll only convince Gwenda that that's the only way it could have been."

Miss Marple's eyes went from him to Gwenda and back again.

"It is a perfectly reasonable hypothesis," she said. "But there is always, as you yourself pointed out, Mr. Reed, the possibility of X."

"X!" said Gwenda.

"The unknown factor," said Miss Marple. "Someone, shall we say, who hasn't appeared yet—but whose presence, behind the obvious facts, can be deduced."

"We're going to the sanatorium in Norfolk where my father died," said Gwenda. "Perhaps we'll find out something there."

10

A Case History

Saltmarsh House was set pleasantly about six miles inland from the coast. It had a good train service to London from the five-mile-distant town of South Benham.

Giles and Gwenda were shown into a large airy sitting room with cretonne covers patterned with flowers. A very charming-looking old lady with white hair came into the room holding a glass of milk. She nodded to them and sat down near the fireplace. Her eyes rested thoughtfully on Gwenda and presently she leaned forward towards her and spoke in what was almost a whisper.

"Is it your poor child, my dear?"

Gwenda looked slightly taken aback. She said doubtfully:

"No—no. It isn't."

"Ah, I wondered." The old lady nodded her head and sipped her milk. Then she said conversationally:

"Half-past ten—that's the time. It's always at half-past ten. Most remarkable." She lowered her voice and leaned forward again.

"Behind the fireplace," she breathed. "But don't say *I* told you."

At this moment, a white-uniformed maid came into the room and requested Giles and Gwenda to follow her.

They were shown into Dr. Penrose's study, and Dr. Penrose rose to greet them.

Dr. Penrose, Gwenda could not help thinking, looked a little mad himself. He looked, for instance, much madder than the nice old lady in the drawing room—but perhaps psychiatrists always looked a little mad.

"I had your letter, and Dr. Kennedy's," said Dr. Penrose. "And I've been looking up your father's case history, Mrs. Reed. I remembered his case quite well, of course, but I wanted to refresh my memory so that I should be in a position to tell you everything you wanted to know. I understand that you have only recently become aware of the facts?"

Gwenda explained that she had been brought up in New Zealand by her mother's relations and that all she had known about her father was that he had died in a nursing home in England.

Dr. Penrose nodded. "Quite so. Your father's case, Mrs Reed, presented certain rather peculiar features."

"Such as?" Giles asked.

"Well, the obsession—or delusion—was very strong. Major Halliday, though clearly in a very nervous state, was most emphatic and categorical in his assertion that he had strangled his second wife in a fit of jealous rage. A great many of the usual signs in these cases were absent, and I don't mind telling you frankly, Mrs. Reed, that had it not been for Dr. Kennedy's assurance that Mrs. Halliday was actually alive, I should have been prepared, at that time, to take your father's assertion at its face value."

"You formed the impression that he had actually killed her?" Giles asked.

"I said 'At that time.' Later, I had cause to revise my opinion, as Major Halliday's character and mental makeup became more familiar to me. Your father, Mrs. Reed, was most definitely *not* a paranoiac type. He had no delusions of persecution, no impulses of violence. He was a gentle, kindly, and well-controlled individual. He was neither what the world calls mad, nor was he dangerous to others. But he did have this obstinate fixation about Mrs. Halliday's death, and to account for its origin I am quite convinced we have to go back a long way—to some childish experience. But I admit that all methods of analysis failed to give us the right clue. Breaking down a patient's resistance to analysis is sometimes a very long business.

It may take several years. In your father's case, the time was insufficient."

He paused, and then, looking up sharply, said:

"You know, I presume, that Major Halliday committed suicide."

"Oh *no!*" cried Gwenda.

"I'm sorry, Mrs. Reed. I thought you knew that. You are entitled, perhaps, to attach some blame to us on that account. I admit that proper vigilance would have prevented it. But frankly I saw no sign of Major Halliday's being a suicidal type. He showed no tendency to melancholia—no brooding or despondency. He complained of sleeplessness and my colleague allowed him a certain amount of sleeping tablets. While pretending to take them, he actually kept them until he had accumulated a sufficient amount and—"

He spread out his hands.

"Was he so dreadfully unhappy?"

"No. I do not think so. It was more, I should judge, a guilt complex, a desire for a penalty to be exacted. He had insisted at first, you know, on calling in the police, and though persuaded out of that, and assured that he had actually committed no crime at all, he obstinately refused to be wholly convinced. Yet it was proved to him over and over again, and he had to admit that he had no recollection of committing the actual act."

Dr. Penrose ruffled over the papers in front

of him. "His account of the evening in question never varied. He came into the house, he said, and it was dark. The servants were out. He went into the dining room, as he usually did, poured himself out a drink and drank it, then went through the connecting door into the drawing room. After that he remembered nothing—nothing at all, until he was standing in his bedroom looking down at his wife, who was dead—strangled. He knew he had done it—"

Giles interrupted:

"Excuse me, Dr. Penrose, but *why* did he know he had done it?"

"There was no doubt in his mind. For some months past he had found himself entertaining wild and melodramatic suspicions. He told me, for instance, that he had been convinced his wife was administering drugs to him. He had, of course, lived in India, and the practice of wives driving their husbands insane by datura poisoning often comes up there in the native courts. He had suffered fairly often from hallucinations, with confusion of time and place. He denied strenuously that he suspected his wife of infidelity, but nevertheless I think that that was the motivating power. It seems that what actually occurred was that he went into the drawing room, read the note his wife left saying she was leaving him, and that his way of eluding this fact was to prefer to 'kill' her. Hence the hallucination."

"You mean he cared for her very much?" asked Gwenda.

"Obviously, Mrs. Reed."

"And he never—recognized—that it was a hallucination?"

"He had to acknowledge that it *must* be—but his inner belief remained unshaken. The obsession was too strong to yield to reason. If we could have uncovered the underlying childish fixation—"

Gwenda interrupted. She was uninterested in childish fixations.

"But *you're* quite sure, you say, that he—that he didn't do it?"

"Oh, if that is what is worrying you, Mrs. Reed, you can put it right out of your head. Kelvin Halliday, however jealous he may have been of his wife, was emphatically not a killer."

Dr. Penrose coughed and picked up a small shabby black book.

"If you would like this, Mrs. Reed, you are the proper person to have it. It contains various jottings set down by your father during the time he was here. When we turned over his effects to his executor (actually a firm of solicitors), Dr. McGuire, who was then superintendent, retained this as part of the case history. Your father's case,

you know, appears in Dr. McGuire's book—
only under initials, of course. Mr. K. H. If
you would like this diary—"

Gwenda stretched out her hand eagerly.

"Thank you," she said. "I should like it
very much."

II

In the train on the way back to London,
Gwenda took out the shabby little black book
and began to read.

She opened it at random.

Kelvin Halliday had written:

I suppose these doctor wallahs know
their business. . . . It all sounds such
poppycock. Was I in love with my mother?
Did I hate my father? I don't believe a
word of it. . . . I can't help feeling this is
a simple police case—criminal court—not
a crazy loony bin matter. And yet—some
of these people here—so natural, so reasonable—just like everyone else—except
when you suddenly come across the kink.
Very well, then, it seems that I, too, have
a kink. . . .

I've written to James . . . urged him to
communicate with Helen. . . . Let her
come and see me in the flesh if she's
alive. . . . He says he doesn't know where
she is . . . that's because he knows that
she's dead and that I killed her . . . he's a
good fellow, but I'm not deceived. . . .
Helen is dead. . . .

When did I begin to suspect her? A long time ago . . . Soon after we came to Dillmouth . . . Her manner changed . . . She was concealing something . . . I used to watch her . . . Yes, and *she* used to watch *me*. . . .

Did she give me drugs in my food? Those queer awful nightmares. Not ordinary dreams . . . living nightmares . . . I know it was drugs. . . . Only *she* could have done that. . . . Why? . . . There's some man . . . Some man she was afraid of. . . .

Let me be honest. I suspected, didn't I, that she had a lover? There was someone —I know there was someone— She said as much to me on the boat. . . . Someone she loved and couldn't marry. . . . It was the same for both of us . . . I couldn't forget Megan . . . How like Megan little Gwennie looks sometimes. Helen played with Gwennie so sweetly on the boat . . . Helen . . . You are so lovely, Helen. . . .

Is Helen alive? Or did I put my hands round her throat and choke the life out of her? I went through the dining-room door and I saw the note—propped up on the desk, and then—and then—all black— just blackness. But there's no doubt about it. . . . I killed her. . . . Thank God Gwennie's all right in New Zealand. They're good people. They'll love her for Megan's sake. Megan—Megan, how I wish you were here. . . .

It's the best way . . . No scandal . . . The best way for the child. I can't go on. Not year after year I must take the short way out. Gwennie will never know anything

about all this. She'll never know her father
was a murderer. . . .

Tears blinded Gwenda's eyes. She looked
across at Giles, sitting opposite her. But
Giles's eyes were riveted on the opposite
corner.

Aware of Gwenda's scrutiny, he motioned
faintly with his head.

Their fellow passenger was reading an
evening paper. On the outside of it, clearly
presented to their view, was a melodramatic
caption—

WHO WERE THE MEN IN HER LIFE?

Slowly, Gwenda nodded her head. She
looked down again at the diary.

There was someone—I know there was
someone—

11

The Men in Her Life

Miss Marple crossed Sea Parade and walked along Fore Street, turning up the hill by the arcade. The shops here were the old-fashioned ones. A wool and art needlework shop, a confectioner, a Victorian-looking Ladies' Outfitter and Draper and others of the same kind.

Miss Marple looked in at the window of the art needlework shop. Two young assistants were engaged with customers, but an elderly woman at the back of the shop was free.

Miss Marple pushed open the door and went in. She seated herself at the counter and the assistant, a pleasant woman with grey hair, asked, "What can I do for you, madam?"

Miss Marple wanted some pale blue wool to knit a baby's jacket. The proceedings were leisurely and unhurried. Patterns were discussed, Miss Marple looked through various children's knitting books and in the course of it discussed her great-nephews and nieces. Neither she nor the assistant displayed impatience. The assistant had attended to customers such as Miss Marple for many years. She preferred those gentle gossipy rambling old ladies to the impatient rather impolite young mothers who didn't know what they wanted and had an eye for the cheap and showy.

"Yes," said Miss Marple. "I think that will be very nice indeed. And I always find Storkleg so reliable. It really doesn't shrink. I think I'll take an extra two ounces."

The assistant remarked that the wind was very cold today, as she wrapped up the parcel.

"Yes, indeed, I noticed it as I was coming along the front. Dillmouth has changed a good deal. I have not been here for, let me see, nearly nineteen years."

"Indeed, madam? Then you will find a lot of changes. The Superb wasn't built then, I suppose, nor the Southview Hotel?"

"Oh no, it was quite a small place. I was staying with friends. . . . A house called St. Catherine's—perhaps you know it? On the Leahampton road."

But the assistant had only been in Dillmouth a matter of ten years.

Miss Marple thanked her, took the parcel, and went into the draper's next door. Here, again, she selected an elderly assistant. The conversation ran much on the same lines, to an accompaniment of summer vests. This time, the assistant responded promptly.

"That would be Mrs. Findeyson's house."

"Yes—yes. Though the friends I knew had it furnished. A Major Halliday and his wife and a baby girl."

"Oh yes, madam. They had it for about a year, I think."

"Yes. He was home from India. They had a very good cook—she gave me a wonderful recipe for baked apple pudding—and also, I think, for gingerbread. I often wonder what became of her."

"I expect you mean Edith Pagett, madam. She's still in Dillmouth. She's in service now—at Windrush Lodge."

"Then there were some other people—the Fanes. A lawyer, I think he was!"

"Old Mr. Fane died some years ago— young Mr. Fane, Mr. Walter Fane, lives with his mother. Mr. Walter Fane never married. He's the senior partner now."

"Indeed? I had an idea Mr. Walter Fane had gone out to India—tea planting or something."

"I believe he did, madam. As a young man. But he came home and went into the firm after about a year or two. They do all the best business round here—they're very highly thought of. A very nice quiet gentleman, Mr. Walter Fane. Everybody likes him."

"Why, of course," exclaimed Miss Marple.

"He was engaged to Miss Kennedy, wasn't he? And then she broke it off and married Major Halliday."

"That's right, madam. She went out to India to marry Mr. Fane, but it seems as she changed her mind and married the other gentleman instead."

A faintly disapproving note had entered the assistant's voice.

Miss Marple leaned forward and lowered her voice.

"I was always so sorry for poor Major Halliday (I knew his mother) and his little girl. I understand his second wife left him. Ran away with someone. A rather flighty type, I'm afraid."

"Regular flibbertigibbet, she was. And her brother, the doctor, such a nice man. Did my rheumatic knee a world of good."

"Whom did she run away with? I never heard."

"That I couldn't tell you, madam. Some said it was one of the summer visitors. But I know Major Halliday was quite broken up. He left the place and I believe his health gave way. Your change, madam."

Miss Marple accepted her change and her parcel.

"Thank you so much," she said. "I wonder if—Edith Pagett, did you say—still has that nice recipe for gingerbread? I lost it—or rather my careless maid lost it—and I'm so fond of good gingerbread."

"I expect so, madam. As a matter of fact her sister lives next door here, married to Mr. Mountford, the confectioner. Edith usually comes there on her days out and I'm sure Mrs. Mountford would give her a message."

"That's a very good idea. Thank you *so much* for all the trouble you've taken."

"A pleasure, madam, I assure you."

Miss Marple went out into the street.

"A nice old-fashioned firm," she said to herself. "And those vests are really very nice, so it isn't as though I had wasted any money." She glanced at the pale blue enamel watch that she wore pinned to one side of her dress. "Just five minutes to go before meeting those two young things at the Ginger Cat. I hope they didn't find things too upsetting at the sanatorium."

II

Giles and Gwenda sat together at a corner table at the Ginger Cat. The little black notebook lay on the table between them.

Miss Marple came in from the street and joined them.

"What will you have, Miss Marple? Coffee?"

"Yes, thank you—no, not cakes, just a scone and butter."

Giles gave the order, and Gwenda pushed the little black book across to Miss Marple.

"First you must read that," she said, "and then we can talk. It's what my father—what he wrote himself when he was at the nursing home. Oh, but first of all, just tell Miss Marple exactly what Dr. Penrose said, Giles."

Giles did so. Then Miss Marple opened the little black book and the waitress brought three cups of weak coffee, and a scone and butter, and a plate of cakes. Giles and Gwenda did not talk. They watched Miss Marple as she read.

Finally she closed the book and laid it down. Her expression was difficult to read. There was, Gwenda thought, anger in it. Her lips were pressed tightly together, and her eyes shone very brightly, unusually so, considering her age.

"Yes, indeed," she said. "Yes, indeed!"

Gwenda said:

"You advised us once—do you remember —not to go on? I can see why you did. But we did go on—and this is where we've got to. Only now, it seems as though we'd got to another place where one could—if one liked—stop. . . . Do you think we ought to stop? Or not?"

Miss Marple shook her head slowly. She seemed worried, perplexed.

"I don't know," she said. "I really don't know. It might be better to do so, much better to do so. Because after this lapse of time there is nothing that you can do—nothing, I mean, of a constructive nature."

"You mean that after this lapse of time, there is nothing we can find out?" asked Giles.

"Oh no," said Miss Marple. "I didn't mean that at all. Nineteen years is not such a long time. There are people who would remember things, who could answer questions—quite a lot of people. Servants, for instance. There must have been at least *two* servants in the house at the time, *and* a nurse, and probably a gardener. It will only take time and a little trouble to find and talk to these people. As a matter of fact, I've found *one* of them already. The cook. No, it wasn't that. It was more the question of what practical *good* you can accomplish, and I'd be inclined to say to that—None. And yet—"

She stopped: "There *is* a yet ... I'm a little slow in thinking things out, but I have a feeling that there is something—something perhaps not very tangible—that would be worth taking risks for—even that one *should* take risks for—but I find it difficult to say just what that is. . . ."

Giles began:

"It seems to me—" and stopped.

Miss Marple turned to him gratefully.

"Gentlemen," she said, "always seem to be able to tabulate things so clearly. I'm sure you have thought things out."

"I have been thinking things out," said Giles. "And it seems to me that there are just two conclusions one can come to. One is the same as I suggested before. Helen Halliday wasn't dead when Gwennie saw her lying in the hall. She came to and went away with her lover, whoever he was. That would still fit the facts as we know them. It would square with Kelvin Halliday's rooted belief that he had killed his wife, and it would square with the missing suitcase and clothes and with the note that Dr. Kennedy found. But it leaves certain points unaccounted for. It doesn't explain why Kelvin was convinced he strangled his wife in the *bedroom*. And it doesn't cover the one, to my mind, really staggering question— *Where is Helen Halliday now?* Because it seems to me against all reason that Helen should never have been heard of or from again. Grant that the two letters she wrote are genuine, what happened *after* that? Why did she never write again? She was on affectionate terms with her brother, he's obviously deeply attached to her and always has been. He might disapprove of her conduct, but that doesn't mean that he expected never to hear from her again. And if you ask me, that point has obviously been worrying Kennedy himself. Let's say he accepted at the time absolutely the story he's told us. His sister's going off and Kelvin's breakdown. But he didn't expect never to hear from his sister again. I think, as the years went on, and he didn't hear, and Kelvin Halliday persisted in his delusion and finally committed suicide, that a terrible doubt began to creep up in his mind. Supposing that Kelvin's story was *true*? That he actually *had* killed Helen? There's no word from her—and surely if she had died somewhere abroad, word would have come to him? I think that explains his eagerness when he saw our advertisement. He hoped that it might lead to some account of where she was or what she had been doing. I'm sure it's absolutely unnatural for someone to disappear as—as completely as Helen seems to have done. That, in itself, is highly suspicious."

"I agree with you," said Miss Marple. "But the alternative, Mr. Reed?"

Giles said slowly:

"I've been thinking out the alternative. It's pretty fantastic, you know, and even rather frightening. Because it involves—how can I put it?—a kind of *malevolence. . . .*"

"Yes," said Gwenda. "Malevolence is just right. Even, I think, something that isn't quite sane. . . ." She shivered.

"That *is* indicated, I think," said Miss Marple. "You know, there's a great deal of— well, *queerness* about—more than people imagine. I have seen some of it. . . ."

Her face was thoughtful.

"There can't be, you see, any *normal* explanation," said Giles. "I'm taking now the fantastic hypothesis that Kelvin Halliday *didn't* kill his wife, but, genuinely *thought* he had done so. That's what Dr. Penrose, who seems a decent sort of bloke, obviously wants to think. His first impression of Halliday was that here was a man who had killed his wife and wanted to give himself up to the police. Then he had to take Kennedy's word for it that that wasn't so, so he had perforce to believe that Halliday was a victim of a complex or a fixation or whatever the jargon is—but he didn't really *like* that solution. He'd had a good experience of the type and Halliday didn't square with it. However, on knowing Halliday better, he became quite genuinely sure that Halliday was not the type of man who would strangle a woman under any provocation. So he accepted the fixation theory, but with misgivings. And that really means that only one theory will fit the case—Halliday was induced to believe that he had killed his wife, *by someone else*. In other words, we've come to X.

"Going over the facts very carefully, I'd say that that hypothesis is at least possible. According to his own account. Halliday came into the house that evening, went into the dining room, took a drink *as he usually did*—and then went into the next room, saw a note on the desk and had a blackout—"

Giles paused and Miss Marple nodded her head in approval. He went on:

"Say it wasn't a blackout—that it was just simply dope—knockout drops in the whisky. The next step is quite clear, isn't it? X had strangled Helen in the hall, but afterwards he took her upstairs and arranged her artistically as a *crime passionnel* on the bed, and that's where Kelvin is when he comes to; and the poor devil, who may have been suffering from jealousy where she's concerned, *thinks that he's done it*. What does he do next? Goes off to find his brother-in-law—on the other side of the town and on foot. And that gives X time to do his next trick. Pack and remove a suitcase of clothes and also remove the body—though what he did with the body," Giles ended vexedly, "beats me completely."

"It surprises me you should say *that*, Mr. Reed," said Miss Marple. "I should say that that problem would present few difficulties. But do please go on."

"'Who were the men in her life?'" quoted Giles. "I saw that in a newspaper as we came back in the train. It set me wondering, because that's really the crux of the matter, isn't it? If there *is* an X, as we believe, all we know about him is that he must have been crazy about her—literally crazy about her."

"And so he hated my father," said Gwenda. "And he wanted him to suffer."

"So that's where we come up against it,"

said Giles. "We know what kind of a girl Helen was—" He hesitated.

"Man mad," supplied Gwenda.

Miss Marple looked up suddenly as though to speak, and then stopped.

"—and that she was beautiful. But we've no clue to what other men there were in her life besides her husband. There may have been any number."

Miss Marple shook her head.

"Hardly that. She was quite young, you know. But you are not quite accurate, Mr. Reed. We do know something about what you have termed 'the men in her life.' There was the man she was going out to marry—"

"Ah yes—the lawyer chap? What was his name?"

"Walter Fane," said Miss Marple.

"Yes. But you can't count him. He was out in Malaya or India or somewhere."

"But was he? He didn't remain a tea planter, you know," Miss Marple pointed out. "He came back here and went into the firm, and is now the senior partner."

Gwenda exclaimed:

"Perhaps he followed her back here?"

"He may have done. We don't know."

Giles was looking curiously at the old lady.

"How did you find all this out?"

Miss Marple smiled apologetically.

"I've been gossiping a little. In shops—and waiting for buses. Old ladies are supposed to be inquisitive. Yes, one can pick up quite a lot of local news."

"Walter Fane," said Giles thoughtfully. "Helen turned him down. That may have rankled quite a lot. Did he ever marry?"

"No," said Miss Marple. "He lives with his mother. I'm going to tea there at the end of the week."

"There's someone else we know about, too," said Gwenda suddenly. "You remember there was somebody she got engaged to, or entangled with, when she left school—someone undesirable, Dr. Kennedy said. I wonder just *why* he was undesirable. . . ."

"That's two men," said Giles. "Either of them may have had a grudge, may have brooded. . . . Perhaps the first young man may have had some unsatisfactory mental history."

"Dr. Kennedy could tell us that," said Gwenda. "Only it's going to be a little difficult asking him. I mean it's all very well for me to go along and ask for news of my stepmother whom I barely remember. But it's going to take a bit of explaining if I want to know about her early love affairs. It seems rather excessive interest in a stepmother you hardly knew."

"There are probably other ways of finding out," said Miss Marple. "Oh yes, I think with time and patience, we can gather the information we want."

"Anyway, we've got two possibilities," said Giles.

"We might, I think, infer a third," said Miss Marple. "It would be, of course, a pure hypothesis, but justified, I think, by the turn of events."

Gwenda and Giles looked at her in slight surprise.

"It is just an inference," said Miss Marple, turning a little pink. "Helen Kennedy went out to India to marry young Fane. Admittedly she was not wildly in love with him, but she must have been fond of him, and quite prepared to spend her life with him. Yet as soon as she gets there, she breaks off the engagement and wires her brother to send her money to get home. Now why?"

"Changed her mind, I suppose," said Giles.

Both Miss Marple and Gwenda looked at him in mild contempt.

"Of course she changed her mind," said Gwenda. "We know that. What Miss Marple means is—why?"

"I suppose girls do change their minds," said Giles vaguely.

"*Under certain circumstances,*" said Miss Marple.

Her words held all the pointed innuendo that elderly ladies are able to achieve with the minimum of actual statement.

"Something he did—" Giles was suggesting vaguely, when Gwenda chipped in sharply.

"Of course," she said. "Another man!"

She and Miss Marple looked at each other with the assurance of those admitted to a freemasonry from which men were excluded.

Gwenda added with certainty:

"On the boat! Going out!"

"Propinquity," said Miss Marple.

"Moonlight on the boat deck," said Gwenda. "All that sort of thing. Only—it must have been serious—not just a flirtation."

"Oh yes," said Miss Marple, "I think it was serious."

"If so, why didn't she marry the chap?" demanded Giles.

"Perhaps he didn't really care for her," Gwenda said slowly. Then shook her head. "No, I think in that case she would still have married Walter Fane. Oh, of course, I'm being stupid. Married man."

She looked triumphantly at Miss Marple.

"Exactly," said Miss Marple. "That's how I should reconstruct it. They fell in love, probably desperately in love. But if he was a married man—with children, perhaps—and probably an honourable type—well, that would be the end of it."

"Only she couldn't go on and marry Walter Fane," said Gwenda. "So she wired her brother and went home. Yes, that all fits. And on the boat home, she met my father . . ."

She paused, thinking it out.

"Not wildly in love," she said. "But attracted . . . and then there was me. They were both unhappy . . . and they consoled each other. My father told her about my mother, and perhaps she told him about the other man . . . Yes—of course—" She flicked over the pages of the diary. *"I know there was someone— She said as much to me on the boat . . . Someone she loved and couldn't marry.* Yes—that's it. Helen and my father felt they were alike—and there was me to be looked after, and she thought she could make him happy—and she even thought, perhaps, that she'd be quite happy herself in the end."

She stopped, nodded violently at Miss Marple, and said brightly:

"That's it."

Giles was looking exasperated.

"Really, Gwenda, you make a whole lot of things up and pretend that they actually happened."

"They did happen. They must have happened. And that gives us a third person for X."

"You mean—?"

"The married man. We don't know what he was like. He mayn't have been nice at all. He may have been a little mad. He may have followed her here—"

"You've just placed him as going out to India."

"Well, people can come back from India, can't they? Walter Fane did. It was nearly a year later. I don't say this man *did* come back, but I say he's a possibility. You keep harping on who the men were in her life. Well, we've got three of them. Walter Fane, and some young man whose name we don't know, and a married man—"

"Whom we don't know exists," finished Giles.

"We'll find out," said Gwenda. "Won't we, Miss Marple?"

"With time and patience," said Miss Marple, "we may find out a great deal. Now for my contribution. As a result of a very fortunate little conversation in the draper's today, I have discovered that Edith Pagett, who was cook at St. Catherine's at the time we are interested in, is still in Dillmouth. Her sister is married to a confectioner here. I think it would be quite natural, Gwenda, for you to want to see her. She may be able to tell us a good deal."

"That's wonderful," said Gwenda. "I've thought of something else," she added. "I'm going to make a new will. Don't look so grave, Giles. I shall still leave my money to you. But I shall get Walter Fane to do it for me."

"Gwenda," said Giles. "Do be careful."

"Making a will," said Gwenda, "is a most

normal thing to do. And the line of approach I've thought up is quite good. Anyway, I want to see him. I want to see what he's like, and if I think that possibly—"

She left the sentence unfinished.

"What surprises me," said Giles, "is that no one else answered that advertisement of ours—this Edith Pagett, for example—"

Miss Marple shook her head.

"People take a long time to make up their minds about a thing like that in these country districts," she said. "They're suspicious. They like to think things over."

12

Lily Kimble

Lily Kimble spread a couple of old newspapers on the kitchen table in readiness for draining the chipped potatoes which were hissing in the pan. Humming tunelessly a popular melody of the day, she leaned forward, aimlessly studying the newsprint spread out before her.

Then suddenly she stopped humming and called:

"Jim—Jim. Listen here, will you?"

Jim Kimble, an elderly man of few words, was washing at the scullery sink. To answer his wife, he used his favourite monosyllable.

"Ar?" said Jim Kimble.

"It's a piece in the paper. 'Will anyone with any knowledge of Helen Spenlove Halliday, née Kennedy, communicate with Messrs. Reed and Hardy, Southampton Row!' Seems to me they might be meaning Mrs. Halliday as I was in service with at St. Catherine's.

Took it from Mrs. Findeyson, they did, she and 'er 'usband. *Her* name was Helen right enough— Yes, and she was sister to Dr. Kennedy, him as always said I ought to have had my adenoids out."

There was a momentary pause as Mrs. Kimble adjusted the frying chips with an expert touch. Jim Kimble was snorting into the roller towel as he dried his face.

"Course it's an old paper, this," resumed Mrs. Kimble. She studied its date. "Nigh on a week or more old. Wonder what it's all about? Think as there's any money in it, Jim?"

Mr. Kimble said "Ar" noncommittally.

"Might be a will or something," speculated his wife. "Powerful lot of time ago."

"Ar."

"Eighteen years or more, I shouldn't wonder. . . . Wonder what they're raking it all up for now? You don't think it could be *police*, do you, Jim?"

"Whatever?" asked Mr. Kimble.

"Well, you know what I always thought," said Mrs. Kimble mysteriously. "Told you at the time, I did, when we was walking out. Pretending that she'd gone off with a feller. That's what they say, husbands, when they do their wives in. Depend upon it, it was murder. That's what I said to you and what I said to Edie, but Edie she wouldn't have it at any price. Never no imagination, Edie hadn't. Those clothes she was supposed to have took away with her—well, they weren't right, if you know what I mean. There was a suitcase gone and a bag, and enough clothes to fill 'em, but they wasn't right, those clothes. And that's when I said to Edie, 'Depend upon it,' I said, 'the master's murdered her and put her in the cellar.' Only not really the cellar, because that Layonee, the Swiss nurse, she saw something. Out of the window. Come to the cinema along of me, she did, though she wasn't supposed to leave the nursery—but there, I said, the child never wakes up—good as gold she was, always, in her bed at night. 'And Madam never comes up to the nursery in the evening,' I says. 'Nobody will know if you slip out with me.' So she did. And when we got in, there was ever such a schemozzle going on. Doctor was there and the master ill and sleeping in the dressing room, and the doctor looking after him, and it was then he asked me about the clothes, and it seemed all right at the time. I thought she'd gone off all right with that fellow she was so keen on—and him a married man, too—and Edie said she did hope and pray we wouldn't be mixed up in any divorce case. What was his name now? I can't remember. Began with an M—or was it an R? Bless us, your memory does go."

Mr. Kimble came in from the scullery and, ignoring all matters of lesser moment, demanded if his supper was ready.

"I'll just drain the chips. . . . Wait, I'll get another paper. Better keep this one. 'Twouldn't be likely to be police—not after all this time. Maybe it's lawyers—and money in it. It doesn't *say* something to your advantage . . . but it might be all the same. . . . Wish I knew who I could ask about it. It says write to some address in London—but I'm not sure I'd like to do a thing like that . . . not to a lot of people in London. . . . What do you say, Jim?"

"Ar," said Mr. Kimble, hungrily eyeing the fish and chips.

The discussion was postponed.

13

Walter Fane

Gwenda looked across the broad mahogany desk at Mr. Walter Fane.

She saw a rather tired-looking man of about fifty, with a gentle nondescript face. The sort of man, Gwenda thought, that you would find it a little difficult to recollect if you had just met him casually. . . . A man who, in modern phrase, lacked personality. His voice, when he spoke, was slow and careful and pleasant. Probably, Gwenda decided, a very sound lawyer.

She stole a glance round the office—the office of the senior partner of the firm. It suited Walter Fane, she decided. It was definitely old-fashioned, the furniture was shabby, but was made of good solid Victorian material. There were deed boxes piled up against the walls—boxes with respectable county names on them. Sir John Vavasour-

Trench. Lady Jessup. Arthur ffoulkes Esq. Deceased.

The big sash window, the panes of which were rather dirty, looked into a square backyard flanked by the solid walls of a seventeenth-century adjoining house. There was nothing smart or up-to-date anywhere, but there was nothing sordid either. It was superficially an untidy office with its piled-up boxes, and its littered desk, and its row of lawbooks leaning crookedly on a shelf—but it was actually the office of someone who knew exactly where to lay his hand upon anything he wanted.

The scratching of Walter Fane's pen ceased. He smiled his slow pleasant smile.

"I think that's all quite clear, Mrs. Reed," he said. "A very simple will. When would you like to come in and sign it?"

Gwenda said whenever he liked. There was no particular hurry.

"We've got a house down here, you know," she said. "Hillside."

Walter Fane said, glancing down at his notes:

"Yes, you gave me the address. . . ."

There was no change in the even tenor of his voice.

"It's a very nice house," said Gwenda. "We love it."

"Indeed?" Walter Fane smiled. "Is it on the sea?"

"No," said Gwenda. "I believe the name has been changed. It used to be St. Catherine's."

Mr. Fane took off his pince-nez. He polished them with a silk handkerchief, looking down at the desk.

"Oh yes," he said. "On the Leahampton road?"

He looked up and Gwenda thought how different people who habitually wear glasses look without them. His eyes, a very pale grey, seemed strangely weak and unfocussed.

"It makes his whole face look," thought Gwenda, "as though he isn't really there."

Walter Fane put on the pince-nez again. He said in his precise lawyer's voice:

"I think you said you did make a will on the occasion of your marriage?"

"Yes. But I'd left things in it to various relatives in New Zealand who have died since, so I thought it would be simpler really to make a new one altogether—especially as we mean to live permanently in this country."

Walter Fane nodded.

"Yes, quite a sound view to take. Well, I think this is all quite clear, Mrs. Reed. Perhaps if you come in the day after tomorrow? Will eleven o'clock suit you?"

"Yes, that will be quite all right."

Gwenda rose to her feet and Walter Fane rose also.

Gwenda said, with exactly the little rush she had rehearsed beforehand:

"I—I asked specially for you, because I think—I mean I believe—that you once knew my—my mother."

"Indeed?" Walter Fane put a little additional social warmth into his manner. "What was her name?"

"Halliday. Megan Halliday. I think—I've been told—that you were once engaged to her?"

A clock on the wall ticked. One two, one two, one two.

Gwenda suddenly felt her heart beating a little faster. What a very *quiet* face Walter Fane had. You might see a house like that— a house with all the blinds pulled down. That would mean a house with a dead body in it. ("What idiotic thoughts you do have, Gwenda!")

Walter Fane, his voice unchanged, unruffled, said:

"No, I never knew your mother, Mrs. Reed. But I was once engaged, for a short period, to Helen Kennedy, who afterwards married Major Halliday as his second wife."

"Oh, I see. How stupid of me. I've got it all wrong. It was Helen—my stepmother. Of course it's all long before I remember. I was only a child when my father's second marriage broke up. But I heard someone say that you'd once been engaged to Mrs. Halliday in

India—and I thought of course it was my own mother—because of India, I mean. . . . My father met her in India."

"Helen Kennedy came out to India to marry me," said Walter Fane. "Then she changed her mind. On the boat going home she met your father."

It was a plain unemotional statement of fact. Gwenda still had the impression of a house with the blinds down.

"I'm so sorry," she said. "Have I put my foot in it?"

Walter Fane smiled—his slow pleasant smile. The blinds were up.

"It's nineteen or twenty years ago, Mrs. Reed," he said. "One's youthful troubles and follies don't mean much after that space of time. So you are Halliday's baby daughter. You know, don't you, that your father and Helen actually lived here in Dillmouth for a while?"

"Oh yes," said Gwenda, "that's really why we came here. I didn't remember it properly, of course, but when we had to decide where we'd live in England, I came to Dillmouth first of all, to see what it was really like, and I thought it was such an attractive place that I decided that we'd park ourselves right here and nowhere else. And wasn't it luck? We've actually got the same house that my people lived in long ago?"

"I remember the house," said Walter Fane.

Again he gave that slow pleasant smile. "You may not remember me, Mrs. Reed, but I rather imagine I used to give you piggybacks once."

Gwenda laughed.

"Did you really? Then you're quite an old friend, aren't you? I can't pretend I remember you—but then I was only about two and a half or three, I suppose. . . . Were you back on leave from India or something like that?"

"No, I'd chucked India for good. I went out to try tea planting—but the life didn't suit me. I was cut out to follow in my father's footsteps and be a prosy unadventurous country solicitor. I'd passed all my law exams earlier, so I simply came back and went straight into the firm." He paused and said: "I've been here ever since."

Again there was a pause and he repeated in a lower voice:

"Yes—ever since. . . ."

But eighteen years, thought Gwenda, isn't really such a long time as all that. . . .

Then, with a change of manner, he shook hands with her and said:

"Since we seem to be old friends, you really must bring your husband to tea with my mother one day. I'll get her to write to you. In the meanwhile, eleven o'clock on Thursday?"

Gwenda went out of the office and down the stairs. There was a cobweb in the angle of the stairway. In the middle of the web was a pale, rather nondescript spider. It didn't look, Gwenda thought, like a real spider. Not the fat juicy kind of spider who caught flies and ate them. It was more like a ghost of a spider. Rather like Walter Fane, in fact.

II

Giles met his wife on the seafront.

"Well?" he asked.

"He was here in Dillmouth at the time," said Gwenda. "Back from India, I mean. Because he gave me piggybacks. But he couldn't have murdered anyone—not possibly. He's much too quiet and gentle. Very nice, really, but the kind of person you never really notice. You know, they come to parties, but you never notice when they leave. I should think he was frightfully upright and all that, and devoted to his mother, and with a lot of virtues. But from a woman's point of view, terribly *dull*. I can see why he didn't cut any ice with Helen. You know, a nice safe person to marry—but you don't really want to."

"Poor devil," said Giles. "And I suppose he was just crazy about her."

"Oh, I don't know. . . . I shouldn't think so, really. Anyway, I'm sure he wouldn't be our malevolent murderer. He's not my idea of a murderer at all."

"You don't really know a lot about murderers, though, do you, my sweet?"

"What do you mean?"

"Well—I was thinking about quiet Lizzie Borden—only the jury said she didn't do it. And Wallace, a quiet man whom the jury insisted did kill his wife, though the sentence was quashed on appeal. And Armstrong, who everybody said for years was such a kind unassuming fellow. I don't believe murderers are ever a special type."

"I really can't believe that Walter Fane—" Gwenda stopped.

"What is it?"

"Nothing."

But she was remembering Walter Fane polishing his eyeglasses and the queer blind stare of his eyes when she had first mentioned St. Catherine's.

"Perhaps," she said uncertainly, "he *was* crazy about her. . . ."

14

Edith Pagett

Mrs. Mountford's back parlour was a comfortable room. It had a round table covered with a cloth, and some old-fashioned armchairs and a stern-looking but unexpectedly well-sprung sofa against the wall. There were china dogs and other ornaments on the mantelpiece, and a framed coloured representation of the Princesses Elizabeth and Margaret Rose. On another wall was the King in Naval uniform, and a photograph of Mr. Mountford in a group of other bakers and confectioners. There was a picture made with shells and a watercolour of a very green sea at Capri. There were a great many other things, none of them with any pretensions to beauty or the higher life; but the net result was a happy, cheerful room where people sat round and enjoyed themselves whenever there was time to do so.

Mrs. Mountford, née Pagett, was short and

round and dark-haired, with a few grey streaks in the dark. Her sister, Edith Pagett, was tall and dark and thin. There was hardly any grey in her hair though she was at a guess round about fifty.

"Fancy now," Edith Pagett was saying. "Little Miss Gwennie. You must excuse me, m'am, speaking like that, but it does take one back. You used to come into my kitchen, as pretty as could be. 'Winnies' you used to say. 'Winnies,' and what you meant was raisins—though why you called them winnies is more than I can say. But raisins was what you meant and raisins it was I used to give you, sultanas, that is, on account of the stones."

Gwenda stared hard at the upright figure and the red cheeks and black eyes, trying to remember—to remember—but nothing came. Memory was an inconvenient thing.

"I wish I could remember—" she began.

"It's not likely that you would. Just a tiny little mite, that's all you were. Nowadays nobody seems to want to go in a house where there's children. I can't see it myself. Children give life to a house, that's what I feel. Though nursery meals are always liable to cause a bit of trouble. But if you know what I mean, m'am, that's the nurse's fault, not the child's. Nurses are nearly always difficult —trays and waiting upon and one thing and another. Do you remember Layonee at all,

Miss Gwennie? Excuse me, Mrs. Reed, I should say?"

"Leonie? Was she my nurse?"

"Swiss girl, she was. Didn't speak English very well, and very sensitive in her feelings. Used to cry a lot if Lily said something to upset her. Lily was house-parlourmaid. Lily Abbott. A young girl and pert in her ways and a bit flighty. Many a game Lily used to have with you, Miss Gwennie. Play peepbo through the stairs."

Gwenda gave a quick uncontrollable shiver.

The stairs ...

Then she said suddenly:

"I remember Lily. She put a bow on the cat."

"There now, fancy you remembering that! On your birthday it was, and Lily she was all for it, Thomas must have a bow on. Took one off the chocolate box, and Thomas was mad about it. Ran off into the garden and rubbed through the bushes until he got it off. Cats don't like tricks being played on them."

"A black and white cat."

"That's right. Poor old Tommy. Caught mice something beautiful. A real proper mouser." Edith Pagett paused and coughed primly. "Excuse me running on like this, m'am. But talking brings the old days back. You wanted to ask me something?"

"I like hearing you talk about the old days," said Gwenda. "That's just what I want to hear about. You see I was brought up by relations in New Zealand and of course they could never tell me anything about—about my father, and my stepmother. She—she was nice, wasn't she?"

"Very fond of you, she was. Oh yes, she used to take you down to the beach and play with you in the garden. She was quite young herself, you understand. Nothing but a girl, really. I often used to think she enjoyed the games as much as you did. You see she'd been an only child, in a manner of speaking. Dr. Kennedy, her brother, was years and years older and always shut up with his books. When she wasn't away at school, she had to play by herself...."

Miss Marple, sitting back against the wall, asked gently:

"You've lived in Dillmouth all your life, haven't you?"

"Oh yes, madam. Father had the farm up behind the hill—Rylands it was always called. He'd no sons, and Mother couldn't carry on after he died, so she sold it and bought the little fancy shop at the end of the High Street. Yes, I've lived here all my life."

"And I suppose you know all about everyone in Dillmouth?"

"Well, of course it used to be a small place

Introducing the first and only complete hardcover collection of Agatha Christie's mysteries

Now you can enjoy the
greatest mysteries ever written
in a magnificent
Home Library Edition.

Discover Agatha Christie's world of mystery, adventure and intrigue

Agatha Christie's timeless tales of mystery and suspense offer something for every reader—mystery fan or not—young and old alike. And now, you can build a complete hardcover library of her world-famous mysteries by subscribing to The Agatha Christie Mystery Collection.

This exciting Collection is your passport to a world where mystery reigns supreme. Volume after volume, you and your family will enjoy mystery reading at its very best.

You'll meet Agatha Christie's world-famous detectives like Hercule Poirot, Jane Marple, and the likeable Tommy and Tuppence Beresford.

In your readings, you'll visit Egypt, Paris, England and other exciting destinations where murder is always on the itinerary. And wherever you travel, you'll become deeply involved in some of the most ingenious and diabolical plots ever invented ... "cliff-hangers" that only Dame Agatha could create!

It all adds up to mystery reading that's so good ... it's almost criminal. And it's yours every month with The Agatha Christie Mystery Collection.

Solve the greatest mysteries of all time. The Collection contains all of Agatha Christie's classic works including *Murder on the Orient Express, Death on the Nile, And Then There Were None, The ABC Murders* and her ever-popular whodunit, *The Murder of Roger Ackroyd.*

Each handsome hardcover volume is Smythe sewn and printed on high quality acid-free paper so it can withstand even the most murderous treatment. Bound in Sussex-blue simulated leather with gold titling, The Agatha Christie Mystery Collection will make a tasteful addition to your living room, or den.

Ride the Orient Express for 10 days without obligation.
To introduce you to the Collection, we're inviting you to examine the classic mystery, *Murder on the Orient Express*, without risk or obligation. If you're not completely satisfied, just return it within 10 days and owe nothing.

However, if you're like the millions of other readers who love Agatha Christie's thrilling tales of mystery and suspense, keep *Murder on the Orient Express* and pay just $9.95 plus postage and handling.

You will then automatically receive future volumes once a month as they are published on a fully returnable, 10-day free-examination basis. No minimum purchase is required, and you may cancel your subscription at any time.

This unique collection is not sold in stores. It's available only through this special offer. So don't miss out, begin your subscription now. Just mail this card today.

☐ Yes! Please send me *Murder on the Orient Express* for a 10-day free-examination and enter my subscription to <u>The Agatha Christie Mystery Collection</u>. If I keep *Murder on the Orient Express*, I will pay just $9.95 plus postage and handling and receive one additional volume each month on a fully returnable 10-day free-examination basis. There is no minimum number of volumes to buy, and I may cancel my subscription at any time. 07013

☐ I prefer the deluxe edition bound in genuine leather for $24.95 per volume plus shipping and handling, with the same 10-day free-examination. 07054

Name_____

Address_____

City_____ State_____ Zip_____

AD12
Send No Money...
But Act Today!

BUSINESS REPLY CARD

FIRST CLASS   PERMIT NO. 2154   HICKSVILLE, N.Y.

Postage will be paid by addressee:

The Agatha Christie
Mystery Collection
Bantam Books
P.O. Box 956
Hicksville, N.Y. 11802

then. Though there used always to be a lot of summer visitors as long as I can remember. But nice quiet people who came here every year, not these trippers and charabancs we have nowadays. Good families they were, who'd come back to the same rooms year after year."

"I suppose," said Giles, "that you knew Helen Kennedy before she was Mrs. Halliday?"

"Well, I knew *of* her, so to speak, and I may have seen her about. But I didn't know her proper until I went into service there."

"And you liked her," said Miss Marple.

Edith Pagett turned towards her.

"Yes, madam, I did," she said. There was a trace of defiance in her manner. "No matter what anybody says. She was as nice as could be to me always. I'd never have believed she'd do what she did do. Took my breath away, it did. Although, mind you, there *had* been talk—"

She stopped rather abruptly and gave a quick apologetic glance at Gwenda.

Gwenda spoke impulsively.

"I want to know," she said. "Please don't think I shall mind anything you say. She wasn't my own mother—"

"That's true enough, m'am."

"And you see, we are very anxious to—to find her. She went away from here—and she seems to have been quite lost sight of. We don't know where she is living now, or even if she is alive. And there are reasons—"

She hesitated and Giles said quickly:

"Legal reasons. We don't know whether to presume death or—or what."

"Oh, I quite understand, sir. My cousin's husband was missing—after Ypres it was—and there was a lot of trouble about presuming death and that. Real vexing it was for her. Naturally, sir, if there is anything I can tell you that will help in any way—it isn't as if you were strangers. Miss Gwenda and her 'winnies.' So funny you used to say it."

"That's very kind of you," said Giles. "So, if you don't mind, I'll just fire away. Mrs. Halliday left home quite suddenly, I understand?"

"Yes, sir, it was a great shock to all of us —and especially to the Major, poor man. He collapsed completely."

"I'm going to ask you right out—have you any idea who the man was she went away with?"

Edith Pagett shook her head.

"That's what Dr. Kennedy asked me—and I couldn't tell him. Lily couldn't either. And of course that Layonee, being a foreigner, didn't know a thing about it."

"You didn't *know*," said Giles. "But could you make a guess? Now that it's all so long ago, it wouldn't matter—even if the guess is all wrong. You must, surely, have had some suspicion."

"Well, we had our suspicions . . . but mind you, it wasn't more than suspicions. And as far as I'm concerned, I never saw anything at all. But Lily who, as I told you, was a sharp kind of girl, Lily had her ideas—had had them for a long time. 'Mark my words,' she used to say. 'That chap's sweet on her. Only got to see him looking at her as she pours out the tea. And does his wife look daggers!'"

"I see. And who was the—er—chap?"

"Now I'm afraid, sir, I just don't remember his name. Not after all these years. A Captain—Esdale—no, that wasn't it—Emery—no. I have a kind of feeling it began with an E. Or it might have been H. Rather an unusual kind of name. But I've never even thought of it for sixteen years. He and his wife were staying at the Royal Clarence."

"Summer visitors?"

"Yes, but I think that he—or maybe both of them—had known Mrs. Halliday before. They came to the house quite often. Anyway, according to Lily he was sweet on Mrs. Halliday."

"And his wife didn't like it."

"No, sir. . . . But mind you, I never believed for a moment that there was anything wrong about it. And I still don't know what to think."

Gwenda asked:

"Were they still here—at the Royal Clarence—when—when Helen—my stepmother went away?"

"As far as I recollect they went away just about the same time, a day earlier or a day later—anyway, it was close enough to make people talk. But I never heard anything definite. It was all kept very quiet if it *was* so. Quite a nine days' wonder Mrs. Halliday going off like that, so sudden. But people did say she'd always been flighty—not that I ever saw anything of the kind myself. I wouldn't have been willing to go to Norfolk with them if I'd thought that."

For a moment three people stared at her intently. Then Giles said:

"Norfolk? Were they going to Norfolk?"

"Yes, sir. They'd bought a house there. Mrs. Halliday told me about three weeks before—before all this happened. She asked me if I'd come with them when they moved, and I said I would. After all, I'd never been away from Dillmouth, and I thought perhaps I'd like a change—seeing as I liked the family."

"I never heard they had bought a house in Norfolk," said Giles.

"Well, it's funny you should say that, sir, because Mrs. Halliday seemed to want it kept very quiet. She asked me not to speak about it to anyone at all—so of course I didn't. But she'd been wanting to go away from Dillmouth for some time. She'd been pressing Major Halliday to go, but he liked it at Dillmouth. I even believe he wrote to Mrs. Findeyson, whom St. Catherine's belonged to, asking if she'd consider selling it. But Mrs. Halliday was dead against it. She seemed to have turned right against Dillmouth. It's almost as though she was afraid to stop there."

The words came out quite naturally, yet at the sound of them the three people listening again stiffened to attention.

Giles said:

"You don't think she wanted to go to Norfolk to be near this—this man whose name you can't remember?"

Edith Pagett looked distressed.

"Oh, indeed, sir, I wouldn't like to think *that*. And I don't think it, not for a moment. Besides, I don't think that—I remember now —they came from up North somewhere, that lady and gentleman did. Northumberland, I think it was. Anyway, they liked coming south for a holiday because it was so mild down here."

Gwenda said:

"She was afraid of something, wasn't she? Or of someone? My stepmother, I mean."

"I do remember—now that you say that—"

"Yes?"

"Lily came into the kitchen one day. She'd

been dusting the stairs, and she said, 'Ructions!' she said. She had a very common way of talking sometimes, Lily had, so you must excuse me.

"So I asked her what she meant and she said that the missus had come in from the garden with the master into the drawing room and the door to the hall being open, Lily'd heard what they said.

"*'I'm afraid of you,*' that's what Mrs. Halliday had said.

"'And she sounded scared too,' Lily said. '*I've been afraid of you for a long time. You're mad. You're not normal. Go away and leave me alone. You must leave me alone. I'm frightened. I think, underneath, I've always been frightened of you. . . .*'

"Something of that kind—of course I can't say now to the exact words. But Lily, she took it very seriously, and that's why, after it all happened, she—"

Edith Pagett stopped dead. A curious frightened look came over her face.

"I didn't mean, I'm sure—" she began. "Excuse me, madam, my tongue runs away with me."

Giles said gently:

"Please tell us, Edith. It's really important, you see, that we should know. It's all a long time ago now, but we've got to *know*."

"I couldn't say, I'm sure," said Edith helplessly.

Miss Marple asked:

"What was it Lily didn't believe—or did believe?"

Edith Pagett said apologetically:

"Lily was always one to get ideas in her head. I never took no notice of them. She was always one for going to the pictures and she got a lot of silly melodramatic ideas that way. She was out at the pictures the night it happened—and what's more she took Layonee with her—and very wrong *that* was, and I told her so. 'Oh, that's all right,' she said. 'It's not leaving the child alone in the house. You're down in the kitchen and the master and the missus will be in later and anyway that child never wakes once she's off to sleep.' But it was wrong, and I told her so, though of course I never knew about Layonee going till afterwards. If I had, I'd have run up to see she—you, I mean, Miss Gwenda—were quite all right. You can't hear a thing from the kitchen when the baize door's shut."

Edith Pagett paused and then went on.

"I was doing some ironing. The evening passed ever so quick and the first thing I knew, Dr. Kennedy came out in the kitchen and asked me where Lily was and I said it was her night off but she'd be in any minute now, and sure enough she came in that very minute and he took her upstairs to the mistress's room. Wanted to know if she'd taken any clothes away with her and what? So Lily looked about and told him and then she come down to me. All agog she was. 'She's hooked it,' she said. 'Gone off with someone. The master's all in. Had a stroke or something. Apparently it's been a terrible shock to him. More fool he. He ought to have seen it coming.' 'You shouldn't speak like that,' I said. 'How do you know she's gone off with anybody? Maybe she had a telegram from a sick relation.' 'Sick relation my foot,' Lily says (always a common way of speaking, as I said). 'She left a note.' 'Who's she gone off with?' I said. 'Who do you think?' Lily said. 'Not likely to be Mr. Sobersides Fane, for all his sheep's eyes and the way he follows her round like a dog.' So I said, 'You think it's Captain—whatever his name was.' And she said, 'He's my bet. Unless it's our mystery man in the flashy car.' (That's just a silly joke we had.) And I said, 'I don't believe it. Not Mrs. Halliday. She wouldn't do a thing like that.' And Lily says, 'Well, it seems she's done it.'

"All this was at first, you understand. But later on, up in our bedroom—Lily woke me up. 'Look here,' she says. 'It's all wrong.' 'What's wrong?' I said. And she said, 'Those clothes.' 'Whatever are you talking about?' I said. 'Listen, Edie,' she said. 'I went through her clothes because the doctor asked me to. And there's a suitcase gone and enough things to fill it—but they're the *wrong* things.' 'What do you mean?' I said. And Lily said, 'She took an evening dress, her grey and silver—but she didn't take her evening belt and brassiere, nor the slip that goes with it, and she took her gold brocade evening shoes, not the silver strap ones. And she took her green tweed—which she never wears until late on in the autumn, but she didn't take that fancy pullover, and she took her lace blouses that she only wears with a town suit. Oh, and her undies, too, they were a job lot. You mark my words, Edie,' Lily said. 'She's not gone away at all. The master's done her in.'

"Well, that made me wide awake. I sat right up and asked her what on earth she was talking about.

"'Just like it was in the *News of the World* last week,' Lily says. 'The master found she'd been carrying on and he killed her and put her down in the cellar and buried her under the floor. You'd never hear anything because it's under the front hall. That's what he's done, and then he packed a suitcase to make it look as though she'd gone away. But that's where she is—under the cellar floor. *She never left this house alive.*' I gave her a piece of my mind then, saying such awful things. But I'll admit I slipped down to the cellar the next morning. But there, it was all just as usual and nothing disturbed and no digging been done—and I went and told Lily she'd just been making a fool of herself, but she stuck to it as the master had done her in. 'Remember,' she says, 'she was scared to death of him. I heard her telling him so.' 'And that's just where you're wrong, my girl,' I said, 'because it wasn't the master at all. Just after you'd told me that day, I looked out of the window and there was the master coming down the hill with his golf clubs, so it couldn't have been him who was with the mistress in the drawing room. It was someone else.'"

The words echoed lingeringly in the comfortable commonplace sitting room.

Giles said softly under his breath:

"*It was someone else....*"

15

An Address

The Royal Clarence was the oldest hotel in
the town. It had a mellow bowfronted fa-
çade and an old-world atmosphere. It still
catered to the type of family who came for
a month to the seaside.

Miss Narracott, who presided behind the
reception desk, was a full-bosomed lady of
forty-seven with an old-fashioned style of
hairdressing.

She unbent to Giles whom her accurate
eye summed up as "one of our nice people."
And Giles, who had a ready tongue and a
persuasive way with him when he liked,
spun a very good tale. He had a bet on
with his wife—about her godmother—and
whether she had stayed at the Royal Clarence eighteen years ago. His wife had said
that they could never settle the dispute because of course all the old registers would
be thrown away by this time, but he had said

"Nonsense." An establishment like the Royal Clarence would keep its registers. They must go back for a hundred years.

"Well, not quite that, Mr. Reed. But we do keep all our old Visitors' Books, as we prefer to call them. Very interesting names in them, too. Why, the King stayed here once when he was Prince of Wales, and Princess Adlemar of Holstein Retz used to come every winter with her lady-in-waiting. And we've had some very famous novelists, too, and Mr. Dovery, the portrait painter."

Giles responded in suitable fashion with interest and respect and in due course the sacred volume for the year in question was brought out and exhibited to him.

Having first had various illustrious names pointed out to him, he turned the pages to the month of August.

Yes, here surely was the entry he was seeking.

Captain and Mrs. Richard Erskine, Anstell Manor, Daith, Northumberland, July 27th—August 17th.

"If I may copy this out?"

"Of course, Mr. Reed. Paper and ink— Oh, you have your pen. Excuse me, I must just go back to the outer office."

She left him with the open book, and Giles set to work.

On his return to Hillside he found Gwenda in the garden bending over the herbaceous border.

She straightened herself and gave him a quick glance of interrogation.

"Any luck?"

"Yes, I think this must be it."

Gwenda said softly, reading the words:

"Anstell Manor, Daith, Northumberland. Yes, Edith Pagett said Northumberland. I wonder if they're still living there—"

"We'll have to go and see."

"Yes—yes, it would be better to go—When?"

"As soon as possible. Tomorrow? We'll take the car and drive up. It will show you a little more of England."

"Suppose they're dead—or gone away and somebody else is living there?"

Giles shrugged his shoulders.

"Then we come back and go on with our other leads. I've written to Kennedy, by the way, and asked him if he'll send me those letters Helen wrote after she went away—if he's still got them—*and* a specimen of her handwriting."

"I wish," said Gwenda, "that we could get in touch with the other servant—with Lily—the one who put the bow on Thomas—"

"Funny your suddenly remembering that, Gwenda."

"Yes, wasn't it? I remember Tommy, too. He was black with white patches and he had three lovely kittens."

"What? Thomas?"

"Well, he was called Thomas—but actually he turned out to be Thomasina. You know what cats are. But about Lily—I wonder what's become of her? Edith Pagett seems to have lost sight of her entirely. She didn't come from round here—and after the breakup at St. Catherine's she took a place in Torquay. She wrote once or twice but that was all. Edith said she'd heard she'd got married but she didn't know who to. If we could get hold of her, we might learn a lot more."

"And from Leonie, the Swiss girl."

"Perhaps—but she was a foreigner and wouldn't catch on to much of what went on. You know, I don't remember her at all. No—it's Lily I feel would be useful. Lily was the sharp one. . . . I know, Giles, let's put in another advertisement—an advertisement for her—Lily Abbott, her name was."

"Yes," said Giles. "We might try that. And we'll definitely go north tomorrow and see what we can find out about the Erskines."

16

Mother's Son

"Down, Henry," said Mrs. Fane to an asthmatic spaniel whose liquid eyes burned with greed. "Another scone, Miss Marple, while they're hot?"

"Thank you. Such delicious scones. You have an excellent cook."

"Louisa is not bad, really. Forgetful, like all of them. And no variety in her puddings. Tell me, how is Dorothy Yarde's sciatica nowadays? She used to be a martyr to it. Largely nerves, I suspect."

Miss Marple hastened to oblige with details of their mutual acquaintance's ailments. It was fortunate, she thought, that among her many friends and relations scattered over England, she had managed to find a woman who knew Mrs. Fane and who had written explaining that a Miss Marple was at present in Dillmouth and would dear Eleanor be very kind and ask her to something.

Eleanor Fane was a tall, commanding woman with a steely grey eye, crisp white hair, and a baby pink and white complexion which masked the fact that there was no babylike softness whatever about her.

They discussed Dorothy's ailments or imagined ailments and went on to Miss Marple's health, the air of Dillmouth, and the general poor condition of most of the younger generation.

"Not made to eat their crusts as children," Mrs. Fane pronounced. "None of that allowed in *my* nursery."

"You have more than one son?" asked Miss Marple.

"Three. The eldest, Gerald, is in Singapore in the Far East Bank. Robert is in the Army." Mrs. Fane sniffed. "Married a Roman Catholic," she said with significance. "You know what *that* means! All the children brought up as Catholics. What Robert's father would have said, I don't know. My husband was very Low Church. I hardly ever hear from Robert nowadays. He takes exception to some of the things I have said to him purely for his own good. I believe in being sincere and saying exactly what one thinks. His marriage was, in my opinion, a great misfortune. He may pretend to be happy, poor boy—but I can't feel that it is at all satisfactory."

"Your youngest son is not married, I believe?"

Mrs. Fane beamed.

"No, Walter lives at home. He is slightly delicate—always was from a child—and I have always had to look after his health very carefully. (He will be in presently.) I can't tell you what a thoughtful and devoted son he is. I am really a very lucky woman to have such a son."

"And he has never thought of marrying?" inquired Miss Marple.

"Walter always says he really cannot be bothered with the modern young woman. They don't appeal to him. He and I have so much in common that I'm afraid he doesn't go out as much as he should. He reads Thackeray to me in the evenings, and we usually have a game of piquet. Walter is a real home bird."

"How very nice," said Miss Marple. "Has he always been in the firm? Somebody told me that you had a son who was out in Ceylon as a tea planter, but perhaps they got it wrong."

A slight frown came over Mrs. Fane's face. She urged walnut cake upon her guest and explained.

"That was as a very young man. One of those youthful impulses. A boy always longs to see the world. Actually, there was a girl at the bottom of it. Girls can be *so* unsettling."

"Oh yes, indeed. My own nephew, I remember—"

Mrs. Fane swept on, ignoring Miss Marple's nephew. She held the floor and was enjoying the opportunity to reminisce to this sympathetic friend of dear Dorothy's.

"A *most* unsuitable girl—as seems always to be the way. Oh, I don't mean an *actress* or anything like that. The local doctor's sister—more like his daughter, really, years younger—and the poor man with no idea how to bring her up. Men are so helpless, aren't they? She ran quite wild, entangled herself first with a young man in the office— a mere clerk—and a very unsatisfactory character, too. They had to get rid of him. Repeated confidential information. Anyway, this girl, Helen Kennedy, was, I suppose, very pretty. *I* didn't think so. I always thought her hair was touched up. But Walter, poor boy, fell very much in love with her. As I say, quite unsuitable, no money and no prospects, and not the kind of girl one wanted as a daughter-in-law. Still, what can a mother do? Walter proposed to her and she refused him, and then he got this silly idea into his head of going out to India and being a tea planter. My husband said: 'Let him go,' though of course he was very disappointed. He had been looking forward to having Walter with him in the firm and Walter had passed all his law exams and everything. Still, there it was. Really, the havoc these young women cause!"

"Oh, I know. My nephew—"

Once again Mrs. Fane swept over Miss Marple's nephew.

"So the dear boy went out to Assam or was it Bangalore—really, I can't remember after all these years. And I felt most upset because I knew his health wouldn't stand it. And he hadn't been out there a year (doing very well, too; Walter does everything well) than would you believe it, this impudent chit of a girl changes her mind and writes out that she'd like to marry him after all."

"Dear, dear." Miss Marple shook her head.

"Gets together her trousseau, books her passage—and what do you think the next move is?"

"I can't imagine!"

Miss Marple leaned forward in rapt attention.

"Has a love affair with a married man, if you please. On the boat going out. A married man with three children, I believe. Anyway there is Walter on the quay to meet her and the first thing she does is to say she can't marry him after all. Don't you call that a wicked thing to do?"

"Oh, I do indeed. It might have completely destroyed your son's faith in human nature."

"It should have shown her to him in her true colours. But there, that type of woman gets away with anything."

"He didn't—" Miss Marple hesitated—

"*resent* her action? Some men would have been terribly angry."

"Walter has always had wonderful self-control. However upset and annoyed Walter may be over anything, he never shows it."

Miss Marple peered at her speculatively.

Hesitantly, she put out a feeler.

"That is because it goes really deep, perhaps? One is really astonished sometimes, with children. A sudden outburst from some child that one has thought didn't care at all. A sensitive nature that can't express itself until it's driven absolutely beyond endurance."

"Ah, it's very curious you should say that, Miss Marple. I remember so well. Gerald and Robert, you know, both hot-tempered and always apt to *fight*. Quite natural, of course, for healthy boys—"

"Oh, quite natural."

"And dear Walter, always so quiet and patient. And then, one day, Robert got hold of his model aeroplane—he'd built it up himself with days of work—so patient and clever with his fingers—and Robert, who was a dear, high-spirited boy but careless, smashed it. And when I came into the schoolroom, there was Robert down on the floor and Walter attacking him with the poker, he'd practically knocked him out—and I simply had all I could do to drag Walter off him. He kept repeating: 'He did it on purpose—

he did it on purpose. I'm going to kill him. . . .'
You know, I was quite frightened. Boys feel
things so intensely, do they not?"

"Yes, indeed," said Miss Marple. Her eyes
were thoughtful.

She reverted to the former topic.

"And so the engagement was finally
broken off. What happened to the girl?"

"She came home. Had another love affair
on the way back, and this time married the
man. A widower with one child. A man who
has just lost his wife is always a fair target
—helpless, poor fellow. She married him and
they settled down here in a house the other
side of the town—St. Catherine's—next door
to the hospital. It didn't last, of course—she
left him within the year. Went off with some
man or other."

"Dear, dear!" Miss Marple shook her head.
"What a lucky escape your son had!"

"That's what I always tell him."

"And did he give up tea planting because
his health wouldn't stand it?"

A slight frown appeared on Mrs. Fane's
brow.

"The life wasn't really congenial to him,"
she said. "He came home about six months
after the girl did."

"It must have been rather awkward," ven-
tured Miss Marple. "If the young woman was
actually living here. In the same town—"

"Walter was wonderful," said Walter's

mother. "He behaved exactly as though nothing had happened. I should have thought myself (indeed I said so at the time) that it would be advisable to make a clean break—after all, meetings could only be awkward for both parties. But Walter insisted on going out of his way to be friendly. He used to call at the house in the most informal fashion, and play with the child— Rather curious, by the way, the child's come back here. She's grown-up now, with a husband. Came into Walter's office to make her will the other day. Reed, that's her name now. Reed."

"Mr. and Mrs. Reed? I know them. Such a nice unaffected young couple. Fancy that now—and she is actually the child—"

"The first wife's child. The first wife died out in India. Poor Major—I've forgotten his name—Hallway—something like that—was completely broken up when that minx left him. Why the worst women should always attract the best men is something hard to fathom!"

"And the young man who was originally entangled with her? A clerk, I think you said, in your son's office. What happened to him?"

"Did very well for himself. He runs a lot of these coach tours. Daffodil Coaches. Afflick's Daffodil Coaches. Painted bright yellow. It's a vulgar world nowadays."

"Afflick?" said Miss Marple.

"Jackie Afflick. A nasty pushing fellow.

Always determined to get on, I imagine. Probably why he took up with Helen Kennedy in the first place. Doctor's sister and all that—thought it would better his social position."

"And this Helen has never come back again to Dillmouth?"

"No. Good riddance. Probably gone completely to the bad by now. I was sorry for Dr. Kennedy. Not his fault. His father's second wife was a fluffy little thing, years younger than he was. Helen inherited her wild blood from her, I expect. I've always thought—"

Mrs. Fane broke off.

"Here is Walter." Her mother's ear had distinguished certain well-known sounds in the hall. The door opened and Walter Fane came in.

"This is Miss Marple, my son. Ring the bell, son, and we'll have some fresh tea."

"Don't bother, Mother. I had a cup."

"Of course we will have fresh tea—and some scones, Beatrice," she added to the parlourmaid who had appeared to take the teapot.

"Yes, madam."

With a slow likeable smile Walter Fane said:

"My mother spoils me, I'm afraid."

Miss Marple studied him as she made a polite rejoinder.

A gentle quiet-looking person, slightly diffident and apologetic in manner—colourless. A very nondescript personality. The devoted type of young man whom women ignore and only marry because the man they love does not return their affection. Walter, who is Always There. Poor Walter, his mother's darling ... Little Walter Fane, who had attacked his older brother with a poker and had tried to kill him. ...

Miss Marple wondered.

17

Richard Erskine

Anstell Manor had a bleak aspect. It was a white house, set against a background of bleak hills. A winding drive led up through dense shrubbery.

Giles said to Gwenda:

"Why have we come? What can we possibly say?"

"We've got it worked out."

"Yes—so far as that goes. It's lucky that Miss Marple's cousin's sister's aunt's brother-in-law or whatever it was lives near here. . . . But it's a far step from a social call to asking your host about his bygone love affairs."

"And such a long time ago. Perhaps—perhaps he doesn't even remember her."

"Perhaps he doesn't. And perhaps there never was a love affair."

"Giles, are we making unutterable fools of ourselves?"

"I don't know. . . . Sometimes I feel that. I don't see why we're concerning ourselves with all this. What does it matter now?"

"So long after . . . Yes, I know. . . . Miss Marple and Dr. Kennedy both said: 'Leave it alone.' Why don't we, Giles? What makes us go on? Is it *her*?"

"Her?"

"Helen. Is that why I remember? Is my childish memory the only link she's got with life—with truth? Is it Helen who's using me—and you—so that the truth will be known?"

"You mean, because she died a violent death—?"

"Yes. They say—books say—that sometimes they can't rest. . . ."

"I think you're being fanciful, Gwenda."

"Perhaps I am. Anyway, we can—choose. This is only a social call. There's no need for it to be anything more—unless we want it to be—"

Giles shook his head.

"We shall go on. We can't help ourselves."

"Yes—you're right. All the same, Giles, I think I'm rather frightened—"

II

"Looking for a house, are you?" said Major Erskine.

He offered Gwenda a plate of sandwiches. Gwenda took one, looking up at him. Richard

Erskine was a small man, five foot nine or so. His hair was grey and he had tired, rather thoughtful eyes. His voice was low and pleasant with a slight drawl. There was nothing remarkable about him, but he was, Gwenda thought, definitely attractive. . . . He was actually not nearly as good-looking as Walter Fane, but whereas most women would pass Fane without a second glance, they would not pass Erskine. Fane was nondescript. Erskine, in spite of his quietness, had personality. He talked of ordinary things in an ordinary manner, but there was *something*—that something that women are quick to recognize and to which they react in a purely female way. Almost unconsciously Gwenda adjusted her skirt, tweaked at a side curl, retouched her lips. Nineteen years ago Helen Kennedy could have fallen in love with this man. Gwenda was quite sure of that.

She looked up to find her hostess's eyes full upon her, and involuntarily she flushed. Mrs. Erskine was talking to Giles, but she was watching Gwenda, and her glance was both appraising and suspicious. Janet Erskine was a tall woman, her voice was deep—almost as deep as a man's. Her build was athletic; she wore a well-cut tweed with big pockets. She looked older than her husband, but, Gwenda decided, well might not be so. There was a certain haggardness about her face. An unhappy hungry woman, thought Gwenda.

"I bet she gives him hell," she said to herself.

Aloud she continued the conversation.

"House hunting is terribly discouraging," she said. "House agents' descriptions are always glowing—and then, when you actually get there, the place is quite unspeakable."

"You're thinking of settling down in this neighbourhood?"

"Well—this is one of the neighbourhoods we thought of. Really because it's near Hadrian's Wall. Giles has always been fascinated by Hadrian's Wall. You see—it sounds rather odd, I expect, to you—but almost anywhere in England is the same to us. My own home is in New Zealand and I haven't any ties here. And Giles was taken in by different aunts for different holidays and so hasn't any particular ties either. The one thing we don't want is to be too near London. We want the real country."

Erskine smiled.

"You'll certainly find it real country all round here. It's completely isolated. Our neighbours are few and far between."

Gwenda thought she detected an undercurrent of bleakness in the pleasant voice. She had a sudden glimpse of a lonely life— of short dark winter days with the wind whistling in the chimneys—the curtains

drawn—shut in—shut in with that woman
with the hungry unhappy eyes—and neighbours few and far between.

Then the vision faded. It was summer
again, with the French windows open to the
garden—with the scent of roses and the
sounds of summer drifting in.

She said:

"This is an old house, isn't it?"

Erskine nodded.

"Queen Anne. My people have lived here
for nearly three hundred years."

"It's a lovely house. You must be very
proud of it."

"It's rather a shabby house now. Taxation
makes it difficult to keep anything up properly. However, now the children are out in
the world, the worst strain is over."

"How many children have you?"

"Two boys. One's in the Army. The other's
just come down from Oxford. He's going into
a publishing firm."

His glance went to the mantelpiece and
Gwenda's eyes followed his. There was a
photograph there of two boys—presumably
about eighteen and nineteen, taken a few
years ago, she judged. There was pride and
affection in his expression.

"They're good lads," he said, "though I say
it myself."

"They look awfully nice," said Gwenda.

"Yes," said Erskine. "I think it's worth it—

really. Making sacrifices for one's children, I mean," he added in answer to Gwenda's inquiring look.

"I suppose—often—one has to give up a good deal," said Gwenda.

"A great deal sometimes. . . ."

Again she caught a dark undercurrent, but Mrs. Erskine broke in, saying in her deep authoritative voice:

"And you are really looking for a house in this part of the world? I'm afraid I don't know of anything at all suitable round here."

"And wouldn't tell me if you did," thought Gwenda, with a faint spurt of mischief. "That foolish old woman is actually jealous," she thought. "Jealous because I'm talking to her husband and because I'm young and attractive!"

"It depends how much of a hurry you're in," said Erskine.

"No hurry at all really," said Giles cheerfully. "We want to be sure of finding something we really like. At the moment we've got a house in Dillmouth—on the South coast."

Major Erskine turned away from the tea table. He went to get a cigarette box from a table by the window.

"Dillmouth," said Mrs. Erskine. Her voice was expressionless. Her eyes watched the back of her husband's head.

"Pretty little place," said Giles. "Do you know it at all?"

There was a moment's silence, then Mrs. Erskine said in that same expressionless voice:

"We spent a few weeks there one summer —many, many years ago. We didn't care for it—found it too relaxing."

"Yes," said Gwenda. "That's just what we find. Giles and I feel we'd prefer more bracing air."

Erskine came back with the cigarettes. He offered the box to Gwenda.

"You'll find it bracing enough round here," he said. There was a certain grimness in his voice.

Gwenda looked up at him as he lighted her cigarette for her.

"Do you remember Dillmouth at all well?" she asked artlessly.

His lips twitched in what she guessed to be a sudden spasm of pain. In a noncommittal voice he answered:

"Quite fairly well, I think. We stayed—let me see—at the Royal George—no, Royal Clarence Hotel."

"Oh yes, that's the nice old-fashioned one. Our house is quite near there. Hillside it's called, but it used to be called St.—St.— Mary's, was it, Giles?"

"St. Catherine's," said Giles.

This time there was no mistaking the reaction. Erskine turned sharply away, Mrs. Erskine's cup clattered on her saucer.

"Perhaps," she said abruptly, "you would like to see the garden."

"Oh yes, please."

They went out through the French windows. It was a well-kept, well-stocked garden, with a long border and flagged walks. The care of it was principally Major Erskine's, so Gwenda gathered. Talking to her about roses, about herbaceous plants, Erskine's dark, sad face lit up. Gardening was clearly his enthusiasm.

When they finally took their leave and were driving away in the car, Giles asked hesitantly:

"Did you—did you drop it?"

Gwenda nodded.

"By the second clump of delphiniums." She looked down at her finger and twisted the wedding ring on it absently.

"And supposing you never find it again?"

"Well, it's not my real engagement ring. I wouldn't risk *that*."

"I'm glad to hear it."

"I'm very, very sentimental about that ring. Do you remember what you said when you put it on my finger? A green emerald because I was an intriguing green-eyed little cat."

"I daresay," said Giles dispassionately,

"that our peculiar form of endearments might sound odd to someone of, say, Miss Marple's generation."

"I wonder what she's doing now, the dear old thing. Sitting in the sun on the front?"

"Up to something—if I know her! Poking here, or prying there, or asking a few questions. I hope she doesn't ask too many one of these days."

"It's quite a natural thing to do—for an old lady, I mean. It's not as noticeable as though we did it."

Giles's face sobered again.

"That's why I don't like—" He broke off. "It's you having to do it that I mind. I can't bear the feeling that I sit at home and send you out to do the dirty work."

Gwenda ran a finger down his worried cheek.

"I know, darling, I know. But you must admit, it's tricky. It's impertinent to catechize a man about his past love affairs—but it's the kind of impertinence a woman can just get away with—if she's clever. And I mean to be clever."

"I know you're clever. But if Erskine is the man we are looking for—"

Gwenda said meditatively:

"I don't think he is."

"You mean we're barking up the wrong tree?"

"Not entirely. I think he was in love with

Helen all right. But he's *nice*, Giles; awfully nice. Not the strangling kind at all."

"You haven't an awful lot of experience of the strangling kind, have you, Gwenda?"

"No. But I've got my woman's instinct."

"I daresay that's what a strangler's victims often say. No, Gwenda, joking apart, do be careful, won't you?"

"Of course. I feel so sorry for the poor man—that dragon of a wife. I bet he's had a miserable life."

"She's an odd woman. . . . Rather alarming somehow."

"Yes, quite sinister. Did you see how she watched me all the time?"

"I hope the plan will go off all right."

III

The plan was put into execution the following morning.

Giles, feeling, as he put it, rather like a shady detective in a divorce suit, took up his position at a point of vantage overlooking the front gate of Anstell Manor. About half-past eleven he reported to Gwenda that all had gone well. Mrs. Erskine had left in a small Austin car, clearly bound for the market town three miles away. The coast was clear.

Gwenda drove up to the front door and rang the bell. She asked for Mrs. Erskine and was told she was out. She then asked for

Major Erskine. Major Erskine was in the garden. He straightened up from operations on a flower bed as Gwenda approached.

"I'm so sorry to bother you," said Gwenda. "But I think I must have dropped a ring somewhere out here yesterday. I know I had it when we came out from tea. It's rather loose, but I couldn't bear to lose it because it's my engagement ring."

The hunt was soon under way. Gwenda retraced her steps of yesterday, tried to recollect where she had stood and what flowers she had touched. Presently the ring came to light near a large clump of delphiniums. Gwenda was profuse in her relief.

"And now can I get you a drink, Mrs. Reed? Beer? A glass of sherry? Or would you prefer coffee, or something like that?"

"I don't want anything—no, really. Just a cigarette—thanks."

She sat down on a bench and Erskine sat down beside her.

They smoked for a few minutes in silence. Gwenda's heart was beating rather fast. No two ways about it. She had got to take the plunge.

"I want to ask you something," she said. "Perhaps you'll think it terribly impertinent of me. But I want to know dreadfully—and you're probably the only person who could tell me. I believe you were once in love with my stepmother."

He turned an astonished face towards her.

"With your stepmother?"

"Yes. Helen Kennedy. Helen Halliday as she became afterwards."

"I see." The man beside her was very quiet. His eyes looked out across the sunlit lawn unseeingly. The cigarette between his fingers smouldered. Quiet as he was, Gwenda sensed a turmoil within that taut figure, the arm of which touched her own.

As though answering some question he had put to himself, Erskine said:

"Letters, I suppose."

Gwenda did not answer.

"I never wrote her many—two, perhaps three. She said she had destroyed them— but women never do destroy letters, do they? And so they came into *your* hands. And you want to know."

"I want to know more about her. I was— very fond of her. Although I was such a small child when—she went away."

"She went away?"

"Didn't you know?"

His eyes, candid and surprised, met hers.

"I've no news of her," he said, "since— since that summer in Dillmouth."

"Then you don't know where she is now?"

"How should I? It's years ago—years. All finished and done with—forgotten."

"Forgotten?"

He smiled rather bitterly.

"No, perhaps not forgotten. . . . You're very perceptive, Mrs. Reed. But tell me about her. She's not—dead, is she?"

A small cold wind sprang up suddenly, chilled their necks and passed.

"I don't know if she is dead or not," said Gwenda. "I don't know anything about her. I thought perhaps *you* might know?"

She went on as he shook his head:

"You see, she went away from Dillmouth that summer. Quite suddenly one evening. Without telling anyone. And she never came back."

"And you thought I might have heard from her?"

"Yes."

He shook his head.

"No. Never a word. But surely her brother —doctor chap—lives in Dillmouth. He must know. Or is he dead too?"

"No, he's alive. But he doesn't know either. You see—they all thought she went away— with somebody."

He turned his head to look at her. Deep sorrowful eyes.

"They thought she went away with *me*?"

"Well, it was a possibility."

"Was it a possibility? I don't think so. It was never that. Or were we fools—conscientious fools who passed up our chance of happiness?"

Gwenda did not speak. Again Erskine turned his head and looked at her.

"Perhaps you'd better hear about it. There isn't really very much to hear. But I wouldn't like you to misjudge Helen. We met on a boat going out to India. One of the children had been ill, and my wife was following on the next boat. Helen was going out to marry a man in the Woods and Forests or something of that kind. She didn't love him. He was just an old friend, nice and kind, and she wanted to get away from home, where she wasn't happy. We fell in love."

He paused.

"Always a bald kind of statement. But it wasn't—I want to make that quite clear—just the usual shipboard love affair. It was serious. We were both—well—shattered by it. And there wasn't anything to be done. I couldn't let Janet and the children down. Helen saw it the same way as I did. If it had been only Janet—but there were the boys. It was all hopeless. We agreed to say good-bye and try and forget."

He laughed, a short mirthless laugh.

"Forget? I never forgot—not for one moment. Life was just a living hell. I couldn't stop thinking about Helen. . . .

"Well, she didn't marry the chap she had been going out to marry. At the last moment, she just couldn't face it. She went home to England and on the way home she met this other man—your father, I suppose. She wrote to me a couple of months later telling me what she had done. He was very unhappy over the loss of his wife, she said, and there was a child. She thought that she could make him happy and that it was the best thing to do. She wrote from Dillmouth. About eight months later my father died and I came into this place. I sent in my papers and came back to England. We wanted a few weeks' holiday until we could get into this house. My wife suggested Dillmouth. Some friend had mentioned it as a pretty place and quiet. She didn't know, of course, about Helen— Can you imagine the temptation? To see her again. To see what this man she had married was like."

There was a short silence, then Erskine said:

"We came and stayed at the Royal Clarence. It was a mistake. Seeing Helen again was hell. . . . She seemed happy enough, on the whole—I don't know. She avoided being alone with me. . . . I didn't know whether she cared still, or whether she didn't. . . . Perhaps she'd got over it. My wife, I think, suspected something. . . . She's—she's a very jealous woman—always has been."

He added brusquely:

"That's all there is to it. We left Dill-mouth—"

"On August seventeenth," said Gwenda.

"Was that the date? Probably. I can't remember exactly."

"It was a Saturday," said Gwenda.

"Yes, you're right. I remember Janet said it might be a crowded day to travel north—but I don't think it was. . . ."

"Please try and remember, Major Erskine. When was the last time you saw my stepmother—Helen?"

He smiled a gentle tired smile.

"I don't need to try very hard. I saw her the evening before we left. On the beach. I'd strolled down there after dinner—and she was there. There was no one else about. I walked up with her to her house. We went through the garden—"

"What time?"

"I don't know . . . Nine o'clock, I suppose."

"And you said good-bye?"

"And we said good-bye." Again he laughed. "Oh, not the kind of good-bye you're thinking of. It was very brusque and curt. Helen said: 'Please go away now. Go quickly. I'd rather not—' She stopped then—and I—I just went."

"Back to the hotel?"

"Yes, yes, eventually. I walked a long way first—right out into the country."

Gwenda said:

"It's difficult with dates—after so many years. But I think that that was the night that she went away—and didn't come back."

"I see. And as I and my wife left the next day, people gossiped and said she'd gone away with me. Charming minds people have."

"Anyway," said Gwenda bluntly, "she didn't go away with you?"

"Good Lord, no. There was never any question of such a thing."

"Then why do you think," asked Gwenda, "that she went away?"

Erskine frowned. His manner changed, became interested.

"I see," he said. "That is a bit of a problem. She didn't—er—leave any explanation?"

Gwenda considered. Then she voiced her own belief.

"I don't think she left any word at all. Do you think she went away with someone else?"

"No, of course she didn't."

"You seem rather sure about that."

"I am sure."

"Then why did she go?"

"If she went off—suddenly—like that—I can only see one possible reason. She was running *away* from me."

"From you?"

"Yes. She was afraid, perhaps, that I'd try to see her again—that I'd pester her. She must have seen that I was still—crazy about her. . . . Yes, that must have been it."

"It doesn't explain," said Gwenda, "why she never came back. Tell me, did Helen say anything to you about my father? That she was worried about him? Or—or afraid of him? Anything like that?"

"Afraid of him? Why? Oh, I see, you thought he might have been jealous. Was he a jealous man?"

"I don't know. He died when I was a child."

"Oh, I see. No—looking back—he always seemed normal and pleasant. He was fond of Helen, proud of her. I don't think more. No, I was the one who was jealous of *him*."

"They seemed to you reasonably happy together?"

"Yes, they did. I was glad—and yet, at the same time, it hurt, to see it. . . . No, Helen never discussed him with me. As I tell you, we were hardly ever alone, never confidential together. But now that you have mentioned it, I do remember thinking that Helen was worried. . . ."

"Worried?"

"Yes. I thought perhaps it was because of my wife—" He broke off. "But it was more than that."

He looked again sharply at Gwenda.

"Was she afraid of her husband? Was he jealous of other men where she was concerned?"

"You seem to think not."

"Jealousy is a very queer thing. It can hide itself sometimes so that you'd never suspect it." He gave a short quick shiver. "But it can be frightening—very frightening. . . ."

"Another thing I would like to know—" Gwenda broke off.

A car had come up the drive. Major Erskine said:

"Ah, my wife has come back from shopping."

In a moment, as it were, he became a different person. His tone was easy yet formal, his face expressionless. A slight tremor betrayed that he was nervous.

Mrs. Erskine came striding round the corner of the house.

Her husband went towards her.

"Mrs. Reed dropped one of her rings in the garden yesterday," he said.

Mrs. Erskine said abruptly:

"Indeed?"

"Good morning," said Gwenda. "Yes, luckily I have found it."

"That's very fortunate."

"Oh, it is. I should have hated to lose it. Well, I must be going."

Mrs. Erskine said nothing. Major Erskine said:

"I'll see you to your car."

He started to follow Gwenda along the terrace. His wife's voice came sharply.

"Richard. If Mrs. Reed will excuse you, there is a very important call—"

Gwenda said hastily:

"Oh, that's quite all right. Please don't bother."

She ran quickly along the terrace and round the side of the house to the drive.

Then she stopped. Mrs. Erskine had drawn up her car in such a way that Gwenda doubted whether she could get her own car past and down the drive. She hesitated, then slowly retraced her steps to the terrace.

Just short of the French windows she stopped dead. Mrs. Erskine's voice, deep and resonant, came distinctly to her ears.

"I don't care what you say. You arranged it—arranged it yesterday. You fixed it up with that girl to come here while I was in Daith. You're always the same—any pretty girl. I won't stand it, I tell you. I won't stand it."

Erskine's voice cut in—quiet, almost despairing.

"Sometimes, Janet, I really think you're insane."

"I'm not the one who's insane. It's *you!* You can't leave women alone."

"You know that's not true, Janet."

"It *is* true! Even long ago—in the place where this girl comes from—Dillmouth. Do you dare tell me that you weren't in love with that yellow-haired Halliday woman?"

"Can you never forget anything? Why must you go on harping on these things. You simply work yourself up and—"

"It's you! You break my heart. . . . I won't stand it, I tell you! I won't stand it! Planning assignations! Laughing at me behind my back! You don't care for me—you've never cared for me. I'll kill myself! I'll throw myself over a cliff— I wish I were dead—"

"Janet—Janet—for God's sake. . . ."

The deep voice had broken. The sound of passionate sobbing floated out into the summer air.

On tiptoe Gwenda crept away and round into the drive again. She cogitated for a moment, then rang the front door bell.

"I wonder," she said, "if there is anyone who—er—could move this car. I don't think I can get out."

The servant went into the house. Presently a man came round from what had been the stableyard. He touched his cap to Gwenda, got into the Austin and drove it into the yard. Gwenda got into her car and drove rapidly back to the hotel, where Giles was waiting for her.

"What a time you've been," he greeted her. "Get anything?"

"Yes. I know all about it now. It's really rather pathetic. He was terribly in love with Helen."

She narrated the events of the morning.

"I really think," she ended, "that Mrs. Erskine is a bit insane. She sounded quite mad. I see now what he meant by jealousy. It must be awful to feel like that. Anyway, we know now that Erskine wasn't the man who went away with Helen, and that he knows nothing about her death. She was alive that evening when he left her."

"Yes," said Giles. "At least—that's what he says."

Gwenda looked indignant.

"That," repeated Giles firmly, "is what he *says*."

18

Bindweed

Miss Marple bent down on the terrace outside the French window and dealt with some insidious bindweed. It was only a minor victory, since beneath the surface the bindweed remained in possession as always. But at least the delphiniums knew a temporary deliverance.

Mrs. Cocker appeared in the drawing-room window.

"Excuse me, madam, but Dr. Kennedy has called. He is anxious to know how long Mr. and Mrs. Reed will be away, and I told him I couldn't take it upon myself to say exactly, but that you might know. Shall I ask him to come out here?"

"Oh. Oh, yes, please, Mrs. Cocker."

Mrs. Cocker reappeared shortly afterwards with Dr. Kennedy.

Rather flutteringly, Miss Marple introduced herself.

"—and I arranged with dear Gwenda that I would come round and do a little weeding while she was away. I think, you know, that my young friends are being imposed upon by their jobbing gardener, Foster. He comes twice a week, drinks a great many cups of tea, does a lot of talking, and not—so far as I can see, very much work."

"Yes," said Dr. Kennedy rather absently. "Yes. They're all alike—all alike."

Miss Marple looked at him appraisingly. He was an older man than she had thought from the Reeds' description of him. Prematurely old, she guessed. He looked, too, both worried and unhappy. He stood there, his fingers caressing the long pugnacious line of his jaw.

"They've gone away," he said. "Do you know for how long?"

"Oh, not for long. They have gone to visit some friends in the North of England. Young people seem to me so restless, always dashing about here and there."

"Yes," said Dr. Kennedy. "Yes—that's true enough."

He paused and then said rather diffidently:

"Young Giles Reed wrote and asked me for some papers—or—letters, if I could find them—"

He hesitated, and Miss Marple said quietly:

"Your sister's letters?"

He shot her a quick, shrewd glance.

"So—you're in their confidence, are you? A relation?"

"Only a friend," said Miss Marple. "I have advised them to the best of my capacity. But people seldom take advice . . . A pity, perhaps, but there it is. . . ."

"What was your advice?" he asked curiously.

"To let sleeping murder lie," said Miss Marple firmly.

Dr. Kennedy sat down heavily on an uncomfortable rustic seat.

"That's not badly put," he said. "I'm fond of Gwennie. She was a nice small child. I should judge that she's grown up to be a nice young woman. I'm afraid that she's heading for trouble."

"There are so many kinds of trouble," said Miss Marple.

"Eh? Yes—yes—true enough."

He sighed. Then he said:

"Giles Reed wrote and asked me if I could let him have my sister's letters, written after she left here—and also some authentic specimen of her handwriting." He shot a keen glance at her. "You see what that means?"

Miss Marple nodded. "I think so."

"They're harking back to the idea that Kelvin Halliday, when he said he had strangled his wife, was speaking neither more nor less than the truth. They believe that the letters

my sister Helen wrote after she went away
weren't written by her at all—that they were
forgeries. They believe that she never left this
house alive."

Miss Marple said gently:

"And you are not, by now, so very sure
yourself?"

"I was at the time." Kennedy still stared
ahead of him. "It seemed absolutely clear.
Pure hallucination on Kelvin's part. There
was no body, a suitcase and clothes were
taken—what else could I think?"

"And your sister had been—recently—
rather—ahem"—Miss Marple coughed delicately—"interested in—in a certain gentleman?"

Dr. Kennedy looked at her. There was deep
pain in his eyes.

"I loved my sister," he said, "but I have to
admit that, with Helen, there was always
some man in the offing. There are women
who are made that way—they can't help it."

"It all seemed clear to you at the time," said
Miss Marple. "But it does not seem so clear
now. Why?"

"Because," said Kennedy with frankness,
"it seems incredible to me that, if Helen is
still alive, she has not communicated with me
all these years. In the same way, if she is
dead, it is equally strange that I have not been
notified of the fact. Well—"

He got up. He took a packet from his pocket.

"Here is the best I can do. The first letter I received from Helen I must have destroyed. I can find no trace of it. But I did keep the second one—the one that gave the poste restante address. And here, for comparison, is the only bit of Helen's handwriting I've been able to find. It's a list of bulbs, and so forth, for planting. A copy that she had kept of some order. The handwriting of the order and the letter look alike to me, but then I'm no expert. I'll leave them here for Giles and Gwenda when they return. It's probably not worth forwarding."

"Oh no, I believe they expect to return tomorrow—or the next day."

The doctor nodded. He stood, looking along the terrace, his eyes still absent. He said suddenly:

"You know what's worrying me? If Kelvin Halliday did kill his wife, he must have concealed the body or got rid of it in some way—and that means (I don't know what else it can mean) that his story to me was a cleverly made-up tale—that he'd already hidden a suitcase full of clothes to give colour to the idea that Helen had gone away—that he'd even arranged for letters to arrive from abroad. . . . It means, in fact, that it was a cold-blooded, premeditated murder. Little

Gwennie was a nice child. It would be bad enough for her to have a father who's a paranoiac, but it's ten times worse to have a father who's a deliberate murderer."

He swung round to the open window. Miss Marple arrested his departure by a swift question.

"Who was your sister afraid of, Dr. Kennedy?"

He turned back to her and stared.

"Afraid of? No one, as far as I know."

"I only wondered. . . . Pray excuse me if I am asking indiscreet questions—but there was a young man, wasn't there—I mean, some entanglement—when she was very young? Somebody called *Afflick*, I believe."

"Oh, that? Silly business most girls go through. An undesirable young fellow, shifty —and of course not her class, not her class at all. He got into trouble here afterwards."

"I just wondered if he could have been— revengeful."

Dr. Kennedy smiled rather skeptically.

"Oh, I don't think it went deep. Anyway, as I say, he got into trouble here, and left the place for good."

"What sort of trouble?"

"Oh, nothing criminal. Just indiscretions. Blabbed about his employer's affairs."

"And his employer was Mr. Walter Fane?"

Dr. Kennedy looked a little surprised.

"Yes—yes—now you say so, I remember,

he did work in Fane and Watchman's. Not articled. Just an ordinary clerk."

Just an ordinary clerk? . . . Miss Marple wondered, as she stooped again to the bindweed after Dr. Kennedy had gone. . . .

19

Mr. Kimble Speaks

"I dunno, I'm sure," said Mrs. Kimble.

Her husband, driven into speech by what was neither more nor less than an outrage, became vocal.

He shoved his cup forward.

"What you thinking of, Lily?" he demanded. *"No sugar!"*

Mrs. Kimble hastily remedied the outrage, and then proceeded to elaborate on her own theme.

"Thinking about this advert, I am," she said. "Lily Abbott it says, plain as plain. And 'formerly house-parlourmaid at St. Catherine's Dillmouth.' That's me, all right."

"Ar," agreed Mr. Kimble.

"After all these years—you must agree it's odd, Jim."

"Ar," said Mr. Kimble.

"Well, what am I going to do, Jim?"

"Leave it be."

"Suppose there's money in it?"

There was a gurgling sound as Mr. Kimble drained his teacup to fortify himself for the mental effort of embarking on a long speech. He pushed his cup along and prefaced his remarks with a laconic "More." Then he got under way.

"You went on a lot at one time about what 'appened at St. Catherine's. I didn't take much account of it—reckoned as it was mostly foolishness—women's chatter. Maybe it wasn't. Maybe something did 'appen. If so, it's police business and you don't want to be mixed up in it. All over and done with, ain't it? You leave well alone, my girl."

"All very well to say that. It may be money as has been left me in a will. Maybe Mrs. Halliday's alive all the time and now she's dead and left me something in 'er will."

"Left you something in 'er will? What for? Ar!" said Mr. Kimble, reverting to his favourite monosyllable to express scorn.

"Even if it's police. . . . You know, Jim, there's a big reward sometimes for anyone as can give information to catch a murderer."

"And what could you give? All you know you made up yourself in your head!"

"That's what you say. But I've been think-ing—"

"Ar," said Mr. Kimble disgustedly.

"Well, I have. Ever since I saw that first piece in the paper. Maybe I got things a bit wrong. That Layonee, she was a bit stupid like all foreigners, couldn't understand proper what you said to her—and her English was something awful. If she didn't mean what I thought she meant . . . I've been trying to remember the name of that man. . . . Now if it was him she saw. . . . Remember that picture I told you about? 'Secret Lover.' Ever so exciting. They tracked him down in the end through his car. Fifty thousand dollars he paid the garage man to forget he filled up with petrol that night. Dunno what that is in pounds. . . . And the other one was there, too, and the husband crazy with jealousy. All mad about her, they were. And in the end—"

Mr. Kimble pushed back his chair with a grating sound. He rose to his feet with slow and ponderous authority. Preparatory to leaving the kitchen, he delivered an ultimatum— the ultimatum of a man who, though usually inarticulate, had a certain shrewdness.

"You leave the whole thing alone, my girl," he said. "Or else, likely as not, you'll be sorry."

He went into the scullery, put on his boots (Lily was particular about her kitchen floor) and went out.

Lily sat on at the table, her sharp, foolish little brain working things out. Of course she couldn't exactly go against what her husband said, but all the same. . . . Jim was so hidebound, so stick-in-the-mud. She wished there was somebody else she could ask—someone who would know all about rewards and the police and what it all meant. Pity to turn up a chance of good money.

That wireless set . . . the home perm . . . that cherry-colour coat in Russell's (ever so smart) . . . even, maybe, a whole Jacobean suite for the sitting room. . . .

Eager, greedy, shortsighted, she went on dreaming. . . . What exactly *had* Layonee said all those years ago?

Then an idea came to her. She got up and fetched the bottle of ink, the pen, and a pad of writing paper.

"Know what I'll do," she said to herself. "I'll write to the doctor, Mrs. Halliday's brother. He'll tell me what I ought to do—if he's alive still, that is. Anyway, it's on my conscience I never told him about Layonee— or about that car."

There was silence for some time apart from the laborious scratching of Lily's pen. It was very seldom that she wrote a letter and she found the composition of it a considerable effort.

However, it was done at last and she put it into an envelope and sealed it up.

But she felt less satisfied than she had expected. Ten to one the doctor was dead or had gone away from Dillmouth.

Was there anyone else?

What was the name, now, of that fellow—

If she could only remember *that*. . . .

20

The Girl Helen

Giles and Gwenda had just finished breakfast on the morning after their return from
Northumberland when Miss Marple was an-
nounced. She came in rather apologetically.

"I'm afraid this is a very early call. Not a
thing I am in the habit of doing. But there
was something I wanted to explain."

"We're delighted to see you," said Giles,
pulling out a chair for her. "Do have a cup
of coffee."

"Oh no, no, thank you—nothing at all. I
have breakfasted *most* adequately. Now let
me explain. I came in whilst you were away,
as you kindly said I might, to do a little
weeding—"

"Angelic of you," said Gwenda.

"And it really did strike me that two days
a week is not quite enough for this garden.
In any case, I think Foster is taking advantage of you. Too much tea and too much talk.

I found out that he couldn't manage another day himself, so I took it upon myself to engage another man just for one day a week—Wednesdays—today, in fact."

Giles looked at her curiously. He was a little surprised. It might be kindly meant, but Miss Marple's action savoured, very faintly, of interference. And interference was unlike her.

He said slowly:

"Foster's far too old, I know, for really hard work."

"I'm afraid, Mr. Reed, that Manning is even older. Seventy-five, he tells me. But you see, I thought employing him, just for a few odd days, might be quite an advantageous move, because he used, many years ago, to be employed at Dr. Kennedy's. The name of the young man Helen got engaged to was Afflick, by the way."

"Miss Marple," said Giles, "I maligned you in thought. You are a genius. You know I've got those specimens of Helen's handwriting from Kennedy?"

"I know. I was here when he brought them."

"I'm posting them off today. I got the address of a good handwriting expert last week."

"Let's go into the garden and see Manning," said Gwenda.

Manning was a bent, crabbed-looking old man with a rheumy and slightly cunning eye. The pace at which he was raking a path accelerated noticeably as his employers drew near.

"Morning, sir. Morning, m'am. The lady said as how you could do with a little extra help of a Wednesday. I'll be pleased. Shameful neglected, this place looks."

"I'm afraid the garden's been allowed to run down for some years."

"It has that. Remember it, I do, in Mrs. Findeyson's time. A picture it were then. Very fond of her garden she was, Mrs. Findeyson."

Giles leaned easily against a roller. Gwenda snipped off some rose heads. Miss Marple, retreating a little upstage, bent to the bindweed. Old Manning leant on his rake. All was set for a leisurely morning discussion of old times and gardening in the good old days.

"I suppose you know most of the gardens round here," said Giles encouragingly.

"Ar, I know this place moderate well, I do. And the fancies people went in for. Mrs. Yule, up at Niagra, she had a yew hedge used to be clipped like a squirrel. Silly, I thought it. Peacocks is one thing and squirrels is another. Then Colonel Lampard, he was a great man for begonias—lovely beds of begonias he used to have. Bedding out now, that's going out of fashion. I wouldn't like to tell you how often I've had to fill up beds in the front lawns and turf 'em over in the last six years. Seems people ain't got no eye for geraniums and a nice bit of lobelia edging no more."

"You worked at Dr. Kennedy's, didn't you?"

"Ar. Long time ago, that were. Must have been nineteen twenty and on. He's moved now—given up. Young Dr. Brent's up at Crosby Lodge now. Funny ideas, he has—little white tablets, and so on. Vittapins he calls 'em."

"I suppose you remember Miss Helen Kennedy, the doctor's sister."

"Ar, I remember Miss Helen right enough. Pretty maid, she was, with her long yellow hair. The doctor set a lot of store by her. Come back and lived in this very house here, she did, after she was married. Army gentleman from India."

"Yes," said Gwenda. "We know."

"Ar. I did 'ear—Saturday night it was—as you and your 'usband was some kind of relations. Pretty as a picter, Miss Helen was, when she first come back from school. Full of fun, too. . Wanting to go everywhere—dances and tennis and all that. 'Ad to mark the tennis court, I 'ad—hadn't been used for nigh twenty years, I'd say. And the shrubs overgrowing it cruel. 'Ad to cut 'em back, I did. *And* get a lot of whitewash and mark out the lines. Lot of work it made—and in the end hardly played on. Funny thing I always thought that was."

"What was a funny thing?" asked Giles.

"Business with the tennis net. Someone come along one night—and cut it to ribbons. Just to ribbons it was. Spite, as you might say. That was what it was—nasty bit of spite."

"But who would do a thing like that?"

"That's what the doctor wanted to know. Proper put out about it he was—and I don't blame him. Just paid for it, he had. But none of us could tell who'd done it. We never did know. And he said he wasn't going to get another—quite right, too, for if it's spite one time, it would be spite again. But Miss Helen, she was rare put out. She didn't have no luck, Miss Helen didn't. First that net—and then her bad foot."

"A bad foot?" asked Gwenda.

"Yes—fell over a scraper or somesuch and cut it. Not much more than a graze, it seemed, but it wouldn't heal. Fair worried about it, the doctor was. He was dressing it and treating it, but it didn't get well. I remember him saying: 'I can't understand it—there must have been something spectic—or some word like that—on that scraper. And anyway,' he says, 'what was the scraper doing out in the middle of the drive?' Because that's where it was when Miss Helen fell over it, walking home on a dark night. The poor maid, there she was, missing going to dances and sitting about with her foot up. Seemed as though there were nothing but bad luck for her."

The moment had come, Giles thought. He asked casually:

"Do you remember somebody called Afflick?"

"Ar. You mean Jackie Afflick? As was in Fane and Watchman's office?"

"Yes. Wasn't he a friend of Miss Helen's?"

"That were just a bit of nonsense. Doctor put a stop to it and quite right too. He wasn't any class, Jackie Afflick. And he was the kind that's too sharp by half. Cut themselves in the end, that kind do. But he weren't here long. Got himself into hot water. Good riddance. Us don't want the likes of he in Dillmouth. Go and be smart somewhere else, that's what he were welcome to do."

Gwenda asked:

"Was he here when that tennis net was cut up?"

"Ar. I see what you're thinking. But he wouldn't do a senseless thing like that. He were smart, Jackie Afflick were. Whoever did that, it was just spite."

"Was there anybody who had a down on Miss Helen? Who would be likely to feel spiteful?"

Old Manning chuckled softly.

"Some of the young ladies might have felt spiteful all right. Not a patch on Miss Helen to look at, most of 'em weren't. No, I'd say that was done just in foolishness. Some tramp with a grudge."

"Was Helen very upset about Jackie Afflick?" asked Gwenda.

"Don't think as Miss Helen cared much about any of the young fellows. Just liked to enjoy herself, that's all. Very devoted some of them were—young Mr. Walter Fane for one. Used to follow her round like a dog."

"But she didn't care for him at all?"

"Not Miss Helen. Just laughed—that's all she did. Went abroad to foreign parts, he did. But he come back later. Top one in the firm he is now. Never married. I don't blame him. Women causes a lot of trouble in a man's life."

"Are you married?" asked Gwenda.

"Buried two, I have," said old Manning. "Ar, well, I can't complain. Smoke me pipe in peace where I likes now."

In the ensuing silence, he picked up his rake again.

Giles and Gwenda walked back up the path towards the house and Miss Marple, desisting from her attack on bindweed, joined them.

"Miss Marple," said Gwenda. "You don't look well. Is there anything—"

"It's nothing, my dear." The old lady paused for a moment before saying with a strange kind of insistence: "You know, I don't like that bit about the tennis net. Cutting it to ribbons. . . . Even then—"

She stopped. Giles looked at her curiously.

"I don't quite understand—" he began.

"Don't you? It seems so horribly plain to me. But perhaps it's better that you shouldn't understand. And anyway—perhaps I am wrong. Now do tell me how you got on in Northumberland."

They gave her an account of their activities, and Miss Marple listened attentively.

"It's really all very sad," said Gwenda. "Quite tragic, in fact."

"Yes, indeed. Poor thing—poor thing."

"That's what I felt. How that man must suffer—"

"He? Oh yes. Yes, of course."

"But you meant—"

"Well, yes—I was thinking of *her*—of the wife. Probably very deeply in love with him, and he married her because she was suitable, or because he was sorry for her, or for one of those quite kindly and sensible reasons that men often have, and which are actually so terribly unfair."

"I know a hundred ways of love,
   And each one makes the loved one rue,"

quoted Giles softly.

Miss Marple turned to him.

"Yes, that is so true. Jealousy, you know, is usually not an affair of *causes*. It is much more—how shall I say?—fundamental than that. Based on the knowledge that one's love is not returned. . . . And so one goes on waiting, watching, expecting . . . that the loved one will turn to someone else. Which, again, invariably happens. So this Mrs. Erskine has made life a hell for her husband, and he, without being able to help it, has made life a hell for her. But I think she has suffered most. And yet, you know, I daresay he is really quite fond of her."

"He can't be," cried Gwenda.

"Oh, my dear, you are very young. He has never left his wife, and that means something, you know."

"Because of the children. Because it was his duty."

"The children, perhaps," said Miss Marple. "But I must confess that gentlemen do not seem to me to have a great regard for duty in so far as their wives are concerned—public service is another matter."

Giles laughed.

"What a wonderful cynic you are, Miss Marple."

"Oh, dear, Mr. Reed, I *do* hope not *that*. One always has *hope* for human nature."

"I still don't feel it can have been Walter Fane," said Gwenda thoughtfully. "And I'm sure it wasn't Major Erskine. In fact I *know* it wasn't."

"One's feelings are not always reliable guides," said Miss Marple. "The most unlikely people do things—quite a sensation there was in my own little village when the treasurer of the Christmas club was found to have put every penny of the funds on a horse. He disapproved of horse racing and indeed any kind of betting or gambling. His father had been a turf agent and had treated his mother very badly—so, intellectually speaking, he was quite sincere. But he chanced one day to be motoring near Newmarket and saw some horses training. And then it all came over him —Blood does tell."

"The antecedents of both Walter Fane and Richard Erskine seem above suspicion," said Giles gravely but with a slight amused twist to his mouth. "But then murder is by way of being an amateur crime."

"The important thing is," said Miss Marple, "that they were *there*. On the spot. Walter Fane was here in Dillmouth. Major Erskine, by his own account, must actually have been with Helen Halliday very shortly before her death—*and* he did not return to his hotel for some time that night."

"But he was quite frank about it. He—"

Gwenda broke off. Miss Marple was looking at her very hard.

"I only want to emphasize," said Miss Marple, "the importance of being *on the spot*." She looked from one to the other of them.

Then she said: "I think you will have no trouble in finding out J. J. Afflick's address. As proprietor of the Daffodil Coaches, it should be easy enough."

Giles nodded. "I'll get onto it. Probably in the telephone directory." He paused. "You think we should go and see him?"

Miss Marple waited for a moment or two, then she said:

"If you do—you must be very careful. Remember what that old gardener just said—Jackie Afflick is smart. . . . Please—*please* be careful. . . ."

21

J. J. Afflick

J. J. Afflick, Daffodil Coaches, Devon & Dorset Tours, etc., had two numbers listed in the telephone book. An office address in Exeter and a private address on the outskirts of that town.

An appointment was made for the following day.

Just as Giles and Gwenda were leaving in the car, Mrs. Cocker ran out and gesticulated. Giles put on the brake and stopped.

"It's Dr. Kennedy on the telephone, sir."

Giles got out and ran back. He picked up the receiver.

"Giles Reed here."

"Morning. I've just received rather an odd letter. From a woman called Lily Kimble. I've been racking my brains to remember who she is. Thought of a patient first—that put me off the scent. But I rather fancy she must be a girl who was in service once at your house.

216

House-parlourmaid at the time we know of. I'm almost sure her name was Lily, though I don't recollect her last name."

"There *was* a Lily. Gwenda remembers her. She tied a bow on the cat."

"Gwennie must have a very remarkable memory."

"Oh, she has."

"Well, I'd like to have a word with you about this letter—not over the phone. Will you be in if I come over?"

"We're just on our way to Exeter. We could drop in on you, if you prefer, sir. It's all on our way."

"Good. That'll do splendidly."

"I don't like to talk too much about all this over the phone," explained the doctor when they arrived. "I always have an idea the local exchanges listen in. Here's the woman's letter."

He spread the letter on the table. It was written on cheap lined paper in an uneducated hand.

Dear sir [Lily Kimble had written]
   Id be grateful if you could give me advise about the enclosed wot i cut out of paper. i been thinking and i talked it over with mr Kimble, but i don't know wots best to do about it. Do you think as it means money or a reword becos i could do with the money im sure but woodnt want the police or anything like that. i offen

hav been thinking about that nite wen mrs Halliday went away and i don't think sir she ever did becos the clothes was wrong. i thort at first the master done it but now im not so sure becos of the car i saw out of the window. A posh car it was and i seen it before but i woodnt like to do anything without asking you furst if it was all rite and not police becos i never hav been mixed up with police and mr Kimble woodnt like it. I could come and see you sir if i may next thursday as its market day and mr Kimble will be out. id be very grateful if you could

yours respectfully
Lily Kimble

"It was addressed to my old house in Dillmouth," said Kennedy, "and forwarded on to me here. The cutting is your advertisement."

"It's wonderful," said Gwenda. "This Lily—you see—she *doesn't* think it was my father who did it!"

She spoke with jubilation. Dr. Kennedy looked at her with tired kindly eyes.

"Good for you, Gwennie," he said gently. "I hope you're right. Now this is what I think we'd better do. I'll answer her letter and tell her to come here on Thursday. The train connection is quite good. By changing at Dillmouth Junction she can get here shortly after four-thirty. If you two will come over that afternoon, we can tackle her all together."

"Splendid," said Giles. He glanced at his

watch. "Come on, Gwenda, we must hurry. We've got an appointment," he explained. "With Mr. Afflick of the Daffodil Coaches, and, so he told us, he's a busy man."

"Afflick?" Kennedy frowned. "Of course! Devon Tours in Daffodil Coaches, horrible great butter-coloured brutes. But the name seemed familiar in some other way."

"Helen," said Gwenda.

"My goodness—not that chap?"

"Yes."

"But he was a miserable little rat. So he's come up in the world?"

"Will you tell me something, sir," said Giles. "You broke up some funny business between him and Helen. Was that—simply— because of his—well, social position?"

Dr. Kennedy gave him a dry glance.

"I'm old-fashioned, young man. In the modern gospel, one man is as good as another. That holds morally, no doubt. But I'm a believer in the fact that there is a state of life into which you are born—and I believe you're happiest staying in it. Besides," he added, "I thought the fellow was a wrong 'un. As he proved to be."

"What did he do exactly?"

"That I can't remember now. It was a case, as far as I can recall, of his trying to cash in on some information obtained through his employment with Fane. Some confidential matter relating to one of their clients."

"Was he—sore about his dismissal?"

Kennedy gave him a sharp glance and said briefly:

"Yes."

"And there wasn't any other reason at all for your disliking his friendship with your sister? You didn't think he was—well—odd in any way?"

"Since you have brought the matter up, I will answer you frankly. It seemed to me, especially after his dismissal from his employment, that Jackie Afflick displayed certain signs of an unbalanced temperament. Incipient persecution mania, in fact. But that does not seem to have been borne out by his subsequent rise in life."

"Who dismissed him? Walter Fane?"

"I have no idea if Walter Fane was concerned. He was dismissed by the firm."

"And he complained that he had been victimized?"

Kennedy nodded.

"I see. . . . Well, we must drive like the wind. Till Thursday, sir."

II

The house was newly built. It was of snowcrete, heavily curved, with a big expanse of window. They were shown in through an opulent hall to a study, half of which was taken up by a big chromium-plated desk.

Gwenda murmured nervously to Giles, "Really, I don't know what we should have done without Miss Marple. We lean upon her at every turn. First her friends in Northumberland and now her vicar's wife's Boys' Club Annual Outing."

Giles raised an admonitory hand as the door opened and J. J. Afflick surged into the room.

He was a stout man of middle age, dressed in a rather violently checked suit. His eyes were dark and shrewd, his face rubicund and good-natured. He looked like the popular idea of a successful bookmaker.

"Mr. Reed? Good morning. Pleased to meet you."

Giles introduced Gwenda. She felt her hand taken in a rather overzealous grip.

"And what can I do for you, Mr. Reed?"

Afflick sat down behind his large desk. He offered cigarettes from an onyx box.

Giles entered upon the subject of the Boys' Club Outing. Old friends of his ran the show. He was anxious to arrange for a couple of days' touring in Devon.

Afflick replied promptly in a businesslike manner—quoting prices and making suggestions. But there was a faintly puzzled look on his face.

Finally he said:

"Well, that's all clear enough, Mr. Reed, and I'll send you a line to confirm it. But this is strictly office business. I understood from my clerk that you wanted a private appointment at my private address?"

"We did, Mr. Afflick. There were actually two matters on which I wanted to see you. We've disposed of one. The other is a purely private matter. My wife here is very anxious to get in touch with her stepmother, whom she has not seen for many years, and we wondered if you could possibly help us."

"Well, if you tell me the lady's name—I gather that I'm acquainted with her?"

"You were acquainted with her at one time. Her name is Helen Halliday and before her marriage she was Miss Helen Kennedy."

Afflick sat quite still. He screwed up his eyes and tilted his chair slowly backwards.

"Helen Halliday—I don't recall . . . Helen Kennedy . . ."

"Formerly of Dillmouth," said Giles.

The legs of Afflick's chair came down sharply.

"Got it," he said. "Of course." His round rubicund face beamed with pleasure. "Little Helen Kennedy! Yes, I remember her. But it's a long time ago. Must be twenty years."

"Eighteen."

"Is it really? Time flies, as the saying goes. But I'm afraid you're going to be disappointed, Mrs. Reed. I haven't seen anything of Helen since that time. Never heard of her, even."

"Oh, dear," said Gwenda. "That's very disappointing. We did so hope you could help."

"What's the trouble?" His eyes flickered quickly from one face to another. "Quarrel? Left home? Matter of money?"

Gwenda said:

"She went away—suddenly—from Dillmouth—eighteen years ago with—with someone."

Jackie Afflick said amusedly:

"And you thought she might have gone away with me? Now why?"

Gwenda spoke boldly:

"Because we heard that you—and she—had once—been—well, fond of each other."

"Me and Helen? Oh, but there was nothing in that. Just a boy and girl affair. Neither of us took it seriously." He added drily, "We weren't encouraged to do so."

"You must think us dreadfully impertinent," began Gwenda, but he interrupted her.

"What's the odds? I'm not sensitive. You want to find a certain person and you think I may be able to help. Ask me anything you please—I've nought to conceal." He looked at her thoughtfully. "So you're Halliday's daughter?"

"Yes. Did you know my father?"

He shook his head.

"I dropped in to see Helen once when I was over at Dillmouth on business. I'd heard she was married and living there. She was civil enough"—he paused—"but she didn't ask me to stay to dinner. No, I didn't meet your father."

Had there, Gwenda wondered, been a trace of rancour in that "She didn't ask me to stay to dinner"?

"Did she—if you remember—seem happy?"

Afflick shrugged his shoulders.

"Happy enough. But there, it's a long time ago. I'd have remembered if she'd looked unhappy."

He added with what seemed a perfectly natural curiosity:

"Do you mean to say you've never heard anything of her since Dillmouth eighteen years ago?"

"Nothing."

"No—letters?"

"There were two letters," said Giles. "But we have some reason to think that she didn't write them."

"You think she didn't write them?" Afflick seemed faintly amused. "Sounds like a mystery on the flicks."

"That's rather what it seems like to us."

"What about her brother, the doctor chap, doesn't he know where she is?"

"No."

"I see. Regular mystery, isn't it? Why not advertise?"

"We have."

Afflick said casually:

"Looks as though she's dead. You mightn't have heard."

Gwenda shivered.

"Cold, Mrs. Reed?"

"No. I was thinking of Helen dead. I don't like to think of her dead."

"You're right there. I don't like to think of it myself. Stunning looks she had."

Gwenda said impulsively:

"You knew her. You knew her well. I've only got a child's memory of her. What was she like? What did people feel about her? What did *you* feel?"

He looked at her for a moment or two.

"I'll be honest with you, Mrs. Reed. Believe it or not, as you like. I was sorry for the kid."

"Sorry?" She turned a puzzled stare on him.

"Just that. There she was—just home from school. Longing for a bit of fun like any girl might, and there was that stiff middle-aged brother of hers with his ideas about what a girl could do and couldn't do. No fun at all, that kid hadn't. Well, I took her about a bit—showed her a bit of life. I wasn't really keen on her and she wasn't really keen on me. She just liked the fun of being a daredevil. Then of course they found out we were meeting and he put a stop to it. Don't blame him really. Cut above me, she was. We weren't engaged or anything of that kind. I meant to marry sometime—but not till I was a good bit older. And I meant to get on and to find a wife who'd help me get on. Helen hadn't any money, and it wouldn't have been a suitable match in any way. We were just good friends with a bit of flirtation thrown in."

"But you must have been angry when the doctor—"

Gwenda paused and Afflick said:

"I was riled, I admit. You don't fancy being told you're not good enough. But there, it's no good being thin-skinned."

"And then," said Giles, "you lost your job."

Afflick's face was not quite so pleasant.

"Fired, I was. Out of Fane and Watchman's. And I've a very good idea who was responsible for that."

"Oh?" Giles made his tone interrogative, but Afflick shook his head.

"I'm not saying anything. I've my own ideas. I was framed—that's all—and I've a very fair idea of who did it. *And* why!" The colour suffused his cheeks. "Dirty work," he said. "Spying on a man—laying traps for him —lying about him. Oh, I've had my enemies all right. But I've never let them get me down. I've always given as good as I got. *And* I don't forget."

He stopped. Suddenly his manner changed back again. He was genial once more.

"So I can't help you, I'm afraid. A little bit of fun between me and Helen—that was all. It didn't go deep."

Gwenda stared at him. It was a clear enough story—but was it true? She wondered. Something jarred—it came to the surface of her mind what that something was.

"All the same," she said, "you looked her up when you came to Dillmouth later."

He laughed.

"You've got me there, Mrs. Reed. Yes, I did. Wanted to show her perhaps that I wasn't down and out just because a long-faced lawyer had pushed me out of his office. I had a nice business and I was driving a posh car and I'd done very well for myself."

"You came to see her more than once, didn't you?"

He hesitated a moment.

"Twice—perhaps three times. Just dropped in."

He nodded with sudden finality.

"Sorry I can't help you."

Giles got up.

"We must apologize for taking up so much of your time."

"That's all right. Quite a change to talk about old times."

The door opened and a woman looked in and apologized swiftly.

"Oh, I'm so sorry—I didn't know you had anyone—"

"Come in, my dear, come in. Meet my wife. This is Mr. and Mrs. Reed."

Mrs. Afflick shook hands. She was a tall,

thin, depressed-looking woman, dressed in rather unexpectedly well-cut clothes.

"Been talking over old times, we have," said Mr. Afflick. "Old times before I met you, Dorothy."

He turned to them.

"Met my wife on a cruise," he said. "She doesn't come from this part of the world. Cousin of Lord Polterham's, she is."

He spoke with pride—the thin woman flushed.

"They're very nice, these cruises," said Giles.

"Very educational," said Afflick. "Now, I didn't have any education to speak of."

"I always tell my husband we must go on one of those Hellenic cruises," said Mrs. Afflick.

"No time. I'm a busy man."

"And we mustn't keep you," said Giles. "Good-bye and thank you. You'll let me know about the quotation for the outing?"

Afflick escorted them to the door. Gwenda glanced back over her shoulder. Mrs. Afflick was standing in the doorway of the study. Her face, fastened on her husband's back, was curiously and rather unpleasantly apprehensive.

Giles and Gwenda said good-bye again and went towards their car.

"Bother, I've left my scarf," said Gwenda.

"You're always leaving something," said Giles.

"Don't look martyred. I'll get it."

She ran back into the house. Through the open door of the study she heard Afflick say loudly:

"What do you want to come butting in for? Never any sense."

"I'm sorry, Jackie. I didn't know. Who are those people and why have they upset you so?"

"They haven't upset me. I—" He stopped as he saw Gwenda standing in the doorway.

"Oh, Mr. Afflick, did I leave a scarf?"

"Scarf? No, Mrs. Reed. It's not here."

"Stupid of me. It must be in the car."

She went out again.

Giles had turned the car. Drawn up by the curb was a large yellow limousine, resplendent with chromium.

"Some car," said Giles.

"'A posh car,'" said Gwenda. "Do you remember, Giles? Edith Pagett when she was telling us what Lily said? Lily had put her money on Captain Erskine, not 'our mystery man in the flashy car.' Don't you see, the mystery man in the flashy car was Jackie Afflick?"

"Yes," said Giles. "And in her letter to the doctor Lily mentioned a 'posh car.'"

They looked at each other.

"He was there—'on the spot,' as Miss Marple would say—on that night. Oh, Giles, I can hardly wait until Thursday to hear what Lily Kimble says."

"Suppose she gets cold feet and doesn't turn up after all?"

"Oh, she'll come. Giles, if that flashy car was there that night—"

"Think it was a yellow peril like this?"

"Admiring my bus?" Mr. Afflick's genial voice made them jump. He was leaning over the neatly clipped hedge behind them. "Little Buttercup, that's what I call her. I've always liked a nice bit of bodywork. Hits you in the eye, doesn't she?"

"She certainly does," said Giles.

"Fond of flowers, I am," said Mr. Afflick. "Daffodils, buttercups, calceolarias—they're all my fancy. Here's your scarf, Mrs. Reed. It had slipped down behind the table. Good-bye. Pleased to have met you."

"Do you think he heard us calling his car a yellow peril?" asked Gwenda as they drove away.

Giles looked slightly uneasy.

"Oh, I don't think so. He seemed quite amiable, didn't he?"

"Yes-es—but I don't think that means much. . . . Giles, that wife of his—she's frightened of him. I saw her face."

"What? That jovial pleasant chap?"

"Perhaps he isn't so jovial and pleasant underneath. . . . Giles, I don't think I like Mr. Afflick. . . . I wonder how long he'd been there

behind us listening to what we were saying.
... Just what did we say?"

"Nothing much," said Giles.

But he still looked uneasy.

22

Lily Keeps
an Appointment

"Well, I'm damned," exclaimed Giles.

He had just torn open a letter that had arrived by the after-lunch post and was staring in complete astonishment at its contents.

"What's the matter?"

"It's the report of the handwriting experts."

Gwenda said eagerly:

"And she *didn't* write that letter from abroad?"

"That's just it, Gwenda. *She did.*"

They stared at each other.

Gwenda said incredulously:

"Then those letters weren't a fake. They were genuine. Helen *did* go away from the house that night. And she *did* write from abroad. And she wasn't strangled at all?"

Giles said slowly:

"It seems so. But it really is very upsetting. I don't understand it. Just as everything seems to be pointing the other way."

"Perhaps the experts are wrong?"

"I suppose they might be. But they seem quite confident. Gwenda, I really don't understand a single thing about all this. Have we been making the most colossal idiots of ourselves?"

"All based on my silly behaviour at the theatre? I tell you what, Giles, let's call round on Miss Marple. We'll have time before we get to Dr. Kennedy's at four-thirty."

Miss Marple, however, reacted rather differently from the way they had expected. She said it was very nice indeed.

"But, darling Miss Marple," said Gwenda, "what do you mean by that?"

"I mean, my dear, that somebody hasn't been as clever as they might have been."

"But how—in what way?"

"Slipped up," said Miss Marple, nodding her head with satisfaction.

"But how?" asked Giles.

"Well, dear Mr. Reed, surely you can see how it narrows the field."

"Accepting the fact that Helen actually wrote the letters—do you mean that she might still have been murdered?"

"I mean that it seemed very important to someone that the letters should actually be in Helen's handwriting."

"I see . . . At least I think I see. There must be certain possible circumstances in which Helen could have been induced to write those particular letters. . . . That would narrow things down. But what circumstances exactly?"

"Oh, come now, Mr. Reed. You're not really thinking. It's perfectly simple, really."

Giles looked annoyed and mutinous.

"It's not obvious to me, I can assure you."

"If you'd just reflect a little—"

"Come on, Giles," said Gwenda. "We'll be late."

They left Miss Marple smiling to herself.

"That old woman annoys me sometimes," said Giles. "I don't know now what the hell she was driving at."

They reached Dr. Kennedy's house in good time.

The doctor himself opened the door to them.

"I've let my housekeeper go out for the afternoon," he explained. "It seemed to be better."

He led the way into the sitting room, where a tea tray with cups and saucers, bread and butter and cakes was ready.

"Cup of tea's a good move, isn't it?" he asked rather uncertainly of Gwenda. "Put this Mrs. Kimble at her ease and all that."

"You're absolutely right," said Gwenda.

"Now what about you two? Shall I introduce you straightaway? Or will it put her off?"

Gwenda said slowly:

"Country people are very suspicious. I believe it would be better if you received her alone."

"I think so too," said Giles.

Dr. Kennedy said:

"If you were to wait in the room next door, and if this communicating door were slightly ajar, you would be able to hear what went on. Under the circumstances of the case, I think that you would be justified."

"I suppose it's eavesdropping, but I really don't care," said Gwenda.

Dr. Kennedy smiled faintly and said:

"I don't think any ethical principle is involved. I do not propose, in any case, to give a promise of secrecy—though I am willing to give my advice if I am asked for it."

He glanced at his watch.

"The train is due at Woodleigh Road at four thirty-five. It should arrive in a few minutes now. Then it will take her about five minutes to walk up the hill."

He walked restlessly up and down the room. His face was lined and haggard.

"I don't understand," he said. "I don't understand in the least what it all means. If Helen never left that house, if her letters to me were forgeries." Gwenda moved sharply —but Giles shook his head at her. The doctor went on: "If Kelvin, poor fellow, didn't kill her, then what on earth did happen?"

"Somebody else killed her," said Gwenda.

"But, my dear child, if somebody else killed

her, why on earth should Kelvin insist that he had done so?"

"Because he thought he had. He found her there on the bed and he thought he had done it. That could happen, couldn't it?"

Dr. Kennedy rubbed his nose irritably.

"How should I know? I'm not a psychiatrist. Shock? Nervous condition already? Yes, I suppose it's possible. But who would want to kill Helen?"

"We think one of three people," said Gwenda.

"Three people? What three people? Nobody could have any possible reason for killing Helen—unless they were completely off their heads. She'd no enemies. Everybody liked her."

He went to the desk drawer and fumbled through its contents.

"Came across this the other day—when I was looking for those letters."

He held out a faded snapshot. It showed a tall schoolgirl in a gym tunic, her hair tied back, her face radiant. Kennedy—a younger, happy-looking Kennedy—stood beside her holding a terrier puppy.

"I've been thinking a lot about her lately," he said indistinctly. "For many years I hadn't thought about her at all—almost managed to forget. . . . Now I think about her all the time. That's *your* doing."

His words sounded almost accusing.

"I think it's *her* doing," said Gwenda.

He wheeled round on her sharply.

"What do you mean?"

"Just that. I can't explain. But it's not really us. It's Helen herself."

The faint melancholy scream of an engine came to their ears. Dr. Kennedy stepped out of the window and they followed him. A trail of smoke showed itself retreating slowly along the valley.

"There goes the train," said Kennedy.

"Coming into the station?"

"No, leaving it." He paused. "She'll be here any minute now."

But the minutes passed and Lily Kimble did not come.

II

Lily Kimble got out of the train at Dillmouth Junction and walked across the bridge to the siding where the little local train was waiting. There were few passengers—a half dozen at most. It was a slack time of day and in any case it was market day at Helchester.

Presently the train started—puffing its way importantly along a winding valley. There were three stops before the terminus at Lonsbury Bay: Newton Langford, Matchings Halt (for Woodleigh Camp), and Woodleigh Bolton.

Lily Kimble looked out of the window with eyes that did not see the lush countryside, but saw instead a Jacobean suite upholstered in jade green . . .

She was the only person to alight at the tiny station of Matchings Halt. She gave up her ticket and went out through the booking office. A little way along the road a signpost with "To Woodleigh Camp" indicated a footpath leading up a steep hill.

Lily Kimble took the footpath and walked briskly uphill. The path skirted the side of a wood; on the other side the hill rose steeply, covered with heather and gorse.

Someone stepped out from the trees and Lily Kimble jumped.

"My, you did give me a start," she exclaimed. "I wasn't expecting to meet you here."

"Gave you a surprise, did I? I've got another surprise for you."

It was very lonely in among the trees. There was no one to hear a cry or a struggle. Actually there was no cry and the struggle was very soon over.

A wood pigeon, disturbed, flew out of the wood. . . .

III

"What can have become of the woman?" demanded Dr. Kennedy irritably.

The hands of the clock pointed to ten minutes to five.

"Could she have lost her way coming from the station?"

"I gave her explicit directions. In any case it's quite simple. Turn to the left when she got out of the station and then take the first road to the right. As I say, it's only a few minutes' walk."

"Perhaps she's changed her mind," said Giles.

"It looks like it."

"Or missed the train," suggested Gwenda.

Kennedy said slowly:

"No, I think it's more likely that she decided not to come after all. Perhaps her husband stepped in. All these country people are quite incalculable."

He walked up and down the room.

Then he went to the telephone and asked for a number.

"Hullo? Is that the station? This is Dr. Kennedy speaking. I was expecting someone by the four thirty-five. Middle-aged country woman. Did anyone ask to be directed to me? Or—what do you say?"

The others were near enough to hear the soft lazy accent of Woodleigh Bolton's one porter.

"Don't think as there could be anyone for you, Doctor. Weren't no strangers on the four thirty-five. Mr. Narracotts from Meadows, and Johnnie Lawes, and old Benson's daughter. Weren't no other passengers at all."

"So she changed her mind," said Dr. Kennedy. "Well, I can offer *you* tea. The kettle's on. I'll go out and make it."

He returned with the teapot and they sat down.

"It's only a temporary check," he said more cheerfully. "We've got her address. We'll go over and see her, perhaps."

The telephone rang and the doctor got up to answer.

"Dr. Kennedy?"

"Speaking."

"This is Inspector Last, Longford Police Station. Were you expecting a woman called Lily Kimble—Mrs. Lily Kimble—to call upon you this afternoon?"

"I was. Why? Has there been an accident?"

"Not what you'd call an accident exactly. She's dead. We found a letter from you on the body. That's why I rang you up. Can you make it convenient to come along to Longford Police Station as soon as possible?"

"I'll come at once."

IV

"Now let's get this quite clear," Inspector Last was saying.

He looked from Kennedy to Giles and Gwenda, who had accompanied the doctor.

Gwenda was very pale and held her hands tightly clasped together. "You were expecting this woman by the train that leaves Dillmouth Junction at four-o-five? And gets to Woodleigh Bolton at four thirty-five?"

Dr. Kennedy nodded.

Inspector Last looked down at the letter he had taken from the dead woman's body. It was quite clear.

Dear Mrs. Kimble, [Dr. Kennedy had written]

I shall be glad to advise you to the best of my power. As you will see from the heading of this letter, I no longer live in Dillmouth. If you will take the train leaving Coombeleigh at 3:30, change at Dillmouth Junction, and come by the Lonsbury Bay train to Woodleigh Bolton, my house is only a few minutes' walk. Turn to the left as you come out of the station, then take the first road on the right. My house is at the end of it on the right. The name is on the gate.

> Yours truly,
> *James Kennedy*

"There was no question of her coming by an earlier train?"

"An earlier train?" Dr. Kennedy looked astonished.

"Because that's what she did. She left Coombeleigh, not at three-thirty but at one-thirty—caught the two-o-five from Dillmouth

Junction and got out, not at Woodleigh Bolton, but at Matchings Halt, the station before it."

"But that's extraordinary!"

"Was she consulting you professionally, Doctor?"

"No. I retired from practice some years ago."

"That's what I thought. You knew her well?"

Kennedy shook his head.

"I hadn't seen her for nearly twenty years."

"But you—er—recognized her just now?"

Gwenda shivered, but dead bodies did not affect a doctor, and Kennedy replied thoughtfully:

"Under the circumstances it is hard to say if I recognized her or not. She was strangled, I presume?"

"She was strangled. The body was found in a copse a short way along the track leading from Matchings Halt to Woodleigh Camp. It was found by a hiker coming down from the Camp at about ten minutes to four. Our police surgeon puts the time of death at between two-fifteen and three o'clock. Presumably she was killed shortly after she left the station. No other passenger got out at Matchings Halt. She was the only person to get out of the train there.

"Now why did she get out at Matchings Halt? Did she mistake the station? I hardly think so. In any case she was two hours early for her appointment with you, and had not come by the train you suggested, although she had your letter with her.

"Now just what was her business with you, Doctor?"

Dr. Kennedy felt in his pocket and brought out Lily's letter.

"I brought this with me. The enclosed cutting is an insertion put in the local paper by Mr. and Mrs. Reed here."

Inspector Last read Lily Kimble's letter and the enclosure. Then he looked from Dr. Kennedy to Giles and Gwenda.

"Can I have the story behind all this? It goes back a long way, I gather?"

"Eighteen years," said Gwenda.

Piecemeal, with additions and parentheses, the story came out. Inspector Last was a good listener. He let the three people in front of him tell things in their own way. Kennedy was dry and factual, Gwenda was slightly incoherent, but her narrative had imaginative power. Giles gave, perhaps, the most valuable contribution. He was clear and to the point, with less reserve than Kennedy, and with more coherence than Gwenda. It took a long time.

Then Inspector Last sighed and summed up.

"Mrs. Halliday was Dr. Kennedy's sister and your stepmother, Mrs. Reed. She disappeared from the house you are at present living in eighteen years ago. Lily Kimble (whose maiden name was Abbott) was a servant (house-parlourmaid) in the house at the time. For some reason Lily Kimble inclines (after the passage of years) to the theory that there was foul play. At the time it was assumed that Mrs. Halliday had gone away with a man (identity unknown). Major Halliday died in a mental establishment fifteen years ago still under the delusion that he had strangled his wife—if it was a delusion—"

He paused.

"These are all interesting but somewhat unrelated facts. The crucial point seems to be, is Mrs. Halliday alive or dead? If dead, when did she die? And what did Lily Kimble know?

"It seems, on the face of it, that she must have known something rather important. So important that she was killed in order to prevent her talking about it."

Gwenda cried:

"But how could anyone possibly know she was going to talk about it—except us?"

Inspector Last turned his thoughtful eyes on her.

"It is a significant point, Mrs. Reed, that she took the two-o-five instead of the four-o-five train from Dillmouth Junction. There must be some reason for that. Also, she got out at the station before Woodleigh Bolton. Why? It seems possible to me that, *after* writing to the doctor, she wrote to someone else, suggesting a rendezvous at Woodleigh Camp, perhaps, and that she proposed after that rendezvous, if it was unsatisfactory, to go on to Dr. Kennedy and ask his advice. It is possible that she had suspicions of some definite person, and she may have written to that person hinting at her knowledge and suggesting a rendezvous."

"Blackmail," said Giles bluntly.

"I don't suppose she thought of it that way," said Inspector Last. "She was just greedy and hopeful—and a little muddled about what she could get out of it all. We'll see, maybe the husband can tell us more."

v

"Warned her, I did," said Mr. Kimble heavily. " 'Don't have nought to do with it,' them were my words. Went behind my back, she did. Thought as she knew best. That were Lily all over. Too smart by half."

Questioning revealed that Mr. Kimble had little to contribute.

Lily had been in service at St. Catherine's before he met her and started walking out with her. Fond of the pictures, she was, and told him that, likely as not, she'd been in a house where there'd been a murder.

"Didn't pay much account, I didn't. All imagination, I thought. Never content with plain fact, Lily wasn't. Long rigmarole she told me, about the master doing in the missus and maybe putting the body in the cellar— and something about a French girl what had looked out of the window and seen something or somebody. 'Don't you pay no attention to foreigners, my girl,' I said. 'One and all they're liars. Not like us.' And when she run on about it, I didn't listen because, mark you, she was working it all up out of nothing. Liked a bit of crime, Lily did. Used to take the *Sunday News* what was running a series about Famous Murderers. Full of it, she was, and if she liked to think she'd been in a house where there was a murder—well, thinking don't hurt nobody. But when she was on at me about answering this advertisement—'You leave it alone,' I says to her. 'It's no good stirring up trouble.' And if she'd done as I told her, she'd be alive today."

He thought for a moment or two.

"Ar," he said. "She'd be alive right now. Too smart by half, that was Lily."

23

Which of Them?

Giles and Gwenda had not gone with Inspector Last and Dr. Kennedy to interview Mr. Kimble. They arrived home about seven o'clock. Gwenda looked white and ill. Dr. Kennedy had said to Giles: "Give her some brandy and make her eat something, then get her to bed. She's had a bad shock."

"It's so awful, Giles," Gwenda kept saying. "So awful. That silly woman, making an appointment with the murderer, and going along so confidently—to be killed. Like a sheep to the slaughter."

"Well, don't think about it, darling. After all, we did know there was someone—a killer."

"No, we didn't. Not a killer *now*. I mean, it was *then*—eighteen years ago. It wasn't, somehow, quite real. . . . It might all have been a mistake."

"Well, this proves that it wasn't a mistake. You were right all the time, Gwenda."

Giles was glad to find Miss Marple at Hillside. She and Mrs. Cocker between them fussed over Gwenda, who refused brandy because she said it always reminded her of channel steamers, but accepted some hot whisky and lemon, and then, coaxed by Mrs. Cocker, sat down and ate an omelette.

Giles would have talked determinedly of other things, but Miss Marple, with what Giles admitted to be superior tactics, discussed the crime in a gentle, aloof manner.

"Very dreadful, my dear," she said. "And of course a great shock, but interesting, one must admit. And of course I am so old that death doesn't shock me as much as it does you—only something lingering and painful like cancer really distresses me. The really vital thing is that this proves definitely and beyond any possible doubt that poor young Helen Halliday was killed. We've thought so all along and now we know."

"And according to you we ought to know where the body is," said Giles. "The cellar, I suppose."

"No, no, Mr. Reed. You remember Edith Pagett said she went down there on the morning after because she was disturbed by what Lily had said, and she found no signs of anything of the kind—and there would be signs, you know—if somebody was really looking for them."

"Then what happened to it? Taken away in a car and thrown over a cliff into the sea?"

"No. Come now, my dears, what struck you first of all when you came here—struck you, Gwenda, I should say? The fact that from the drawing-room window, you had no view down to the sea. Where you felt, very properly, that steps should lead down to the lawn—there was instead a plantation of shrubs. The steps, you found subsequently, had been there originally, but had at some time been transferred to the end of the terrace. Why were they moved?"

Gwenda stared at her with dawning comprehension.

"You mean that *that's* where—"

"There must have been a reason for making the change, and there doesn't really seem to be a sensible one. It is, frankly, a stupid place to have steps down to the lawn. But that end of the terrace is a very quiet place—it's not overlooked from the house except by one window—the window of the nursery, on the first floor. Don't you see, that if you want to bury a body, the earth will be disturbed and there must be a *reason* for it being disturbed. The reason was that it had been decided to move the steps from in front of the drawing room to the end of the terrace. I've learnt already from Dr. Kennedy that Helen Halliday and her husband were very keen on the garden, and did a lot of work in it. The daily gardener they employed used merely to carry out their orders, and if he arrived to find that this change was in progress and some of the flags had already been moved, he would only have thought that the Hallidays had started on the work when he wasn't there. The body, of course, could have been buried at either place, but we can be quite certain, I think, that it is actually buried at the end of the terrace and not in front of the drawing-room window."

"Why can we be sure?" asked Gwenda.

"Because of what poor Lily Kimble said in her letter—that she changed her mind about the body being in the cellar because of what Leonie saw when she looked out of the window. That makes it very clear, doesn't it? The Swiss girl looked out of the nursery window at some time during the night and saw the grave being dug. Perhaps she actually saw who it was digging it."

"And never said anything to the police?"

"My dear, there was no question at the time of a *crime* having occurred. Mrs. Halliday had run away with a lover—that was all that Leonie would grasp. She probably couldn't speak much English anyway. She did mention to Lily, perhaps not at the time, but later, a curious thing she had observed from her window that night, and that stimulated Lily's belief in a crime having occurred. But I've no doubt that Edith Pagett told Lily off for talking nonsense, and the Swiss girl would accept her point of view and would certainly not wish to be mixed up with the police. Foreigners always seem to be particularly nervous about the police when they are in a strange country. So she went back to Switzerland and very likely never thought of it again."

Giles said:

"If she's alive now—if she can be traced—"

Miss Marple nodded her head. "Perhaps."

Giles demanded:

"How can we set about it?"

Miss Marple said:

"The police will be able to do that much better than you can."

"Inspector Last is coming over here tomorrow morning."

"Then I think I should tell him—about the steps."

"And about what I saw—or think I saw—in the hall?" asked Gwenda nervously.

"Yes, dear. You've been very wise to say nothing of that until now. Very wise. But I think the time has come."

Giles said slowly:

"She was strangled in the hall, and then the murderer carried her upstairs and put her on the bed. Kelvin Halliday came in, passed out with doped whisky, and in his turn was carried upstairs to the bedroom. He came to, and thought he had killed her. The murderer must have been watching somewhere near at hand. When Kelvin went off to Dr. Kennedy's, the murderer took away the body, probably hid it in the shrubbery at the end of the terrace, and waited until everybody had gone to bed and was presumably asleep before he dug the grave and buried the body. That means he must have been here, hanging about the house, pretty well all that night?"

Miss Marple nodded.

"He had to be—on the spot. I remember your saying that that was important. We've got to see which of our three suspects fits in best with the requirements. We'll take Erskine first. Now he definitely was on the spot. By his own admission he walked up here with Helen Halliday from the beach at round about nine o'clock. He said good-bye to her. But did he say good-bye to her? Let's say instead that he strangled her."

"But it was all over between them," cried Gwenda. "Long ago. He said himself that he was hardly ever alone with Helen."

"But don't you see, Gwenda, that the way we must look at it now, we can't depend on anything anyone *says*."

"Now I'm so glad to hear you say that," said Miss Marple. "Because I've been a little worried, you know, by the way you two have seemed willing to accept, as actual fact, all the things that people have told you. I'm afraid I have a sadly distrustful nature, but, especially in a matter of murder, I make it a rule to take nothing that is told me as true, unless it is *checked.* For instance, it does seem quite certain that Lily Kimble mentioned the clothes packed and taken away in a suitcase were not the ones Helen Halliday would herself have taken, because not only did Edith Pagett tell us that Lily said so to her, but Lily herself mentioned the fact in her letter to Dr. Kennedy. So that is one *fact.* Dr. Kennedy told us that Kelvin Halliday believed that his wife was secretly drugging him, and Kelvin Halliday in his diary confirms that—so there is another fact—and a very curious fact it is, don't you think? However, we will not go into that now.

"But I would like to point out that a great many of the assumptions you have made have been based upon what has been told you—possibly told you very plausibly."

Giles stared hard at her.

Gwenda, her colour restored, sipped coffee, and leaned across the table.

Giles said:

"Let's check up now on what three people have said to us. Take Erskine first. He says—"

"You've got a down on him," said Gwenda. "It's a waste of time going on about him, because now he's definitely out of it. He couldn't have killed Lily Kimble."

Giles went on imperturbably:

"He says that he met Helen on the boat going out to India and they fell in love, but that he couldn't bring himself to leave his wife and children, and that they agreed they must say good-bye. Suppose it wasn't quite like that. Suppose he fell desperately in love with Helen, and that it was *she* who wouldn't run off with him. Supposing he threatened that if she married anyone else, he would kill her."

"Most improbable," said Gwenda.

"Things like that do happen. Remember what you overheard his wife say to him. You put it all down to jealousy, but it may have been true. Perhaps she *has* had a terrible time with him where women are concerned—he may be a little bit of a sex maniac."

"I don't believe it."

"No, because he's attractive to women. I think, myself, that there is something a little queer about Erskine. However, let's go on with my case against him. Helen breaks off her engagement to Fane and comes home and marries your father and settles down here. And then suddenly, Erskine turns up. He comes down ostensibly on a summer holiday with his wife. That's an odd thing to do, really. He admits he came here to see Helen again. Now let's take it that *Erskine* was the man in the drawing room with her that day when Lily overheard her say she was afraid of him. *'I'm afraid of you—I've always been afraid of you—I think you're mad.'*

"And, because she's afraid, she makes

plans to go and live in Norfolk, but she's very secretive about it. No one is to know. No one is to know, that is, until the Erskines have left Dillmouth. So far that fits. Now we come to the fatal night. What the Hallidays were doing earlier that evening, we don't know—"

Miss Marple coughed.

"As a matter of fact, I saw Edith Pagett again. She remembers that there was early supper that night—seven o'clock—because Major Halliday was going to some meeting —golf club, she thinks it was, or some parish meeting. Mrs. Halliday went out after supper."

"Right. Helen meets Erskine, by appointment, perhaps, on the beach. He is leaving the following day. Perhaps he refuses to go. He urges Helen to go away with him. She comes back here and he comes with her. Finally, in a fit of frenzy he strangles her. The next bit is as we have already agreed. He's slightly mad, he wants Kelvin Halliday to believe it is *he* who has killed her. Later, Erskine buries the body. You remember, he told Gwenda that he didn't go back to the hotel until very late because he was walking about Dillmouth."

"One wonders," said Miss Marple, "what his wife was doing?"

"Probably frenzied with jealousy," said

Gwenda. "And gave him hell when he did get in."

"That's my reconstruction," said Giles. "And it's possible."

"But he couldn't have killed Lily Kimble," said Gwenda, "because he lives in Northumberland. So thinking about him is just a waste of time. Let's take Walter Fane."

"Right. Walter Fane is the repressed type. He seems gentle and mild and easily pushed around. But Miss Marple has brought us one valuable bit of testimony. Walter Fane was once in such a rage that he nearly killed his brother. Admittedly he was a child at the time, but it was startling because he had always seemed such a gentle forgiving nature. Anyway, Walter Fane falls in love with Helen Halliday. Not merely in love, he's crazy about her. She won't have him and he goes off to India. Later, she writes him that she will come out and marry him. She starts. Then comes the second blow. She arrives and promptly jilts him. She has 'met someone on the boat.' She goes home and marries Kelvin Halliday. Possibly Walter Fane thinks that Kelvin Halliday was the original cause of her turning him down. He broods, nurses a crazy jealous hate and comes home. He behaves in a most forgiving, friendly manner, is often at this house, has become apparently a tame cat around the house, the faithful Dobbin. But perhaps

Helen realizes that this isn't true. She gets a glimpse of what is going on below the surface. Perhaps, long ago, she sensed something disturbing in quiet young Walter Fane. She says to him, 'I think I've always been afraid of you.' She makes plans, secretly, to go right away from Dillmouth and live in Norfolk. Why? Because she's afraid of Walter Fane.

"Now we come again to the fatal evening. Here, we're not on very sure ground. We don't know what Walter Fane was doing that night, and I don't see any probability of ever finding out. But he fulfils Miss Marple's requirement of being 'on the spot' to the extent of living in a house that is only two or three minutes' walk away. He may have said he was going to bed early with a headache, or shut himself into his study with work to do —something of that kind. He could have done all the things we've decided the murderer did do, and I think that he's the most likely of the three to have made mistakes in packing a suitcase. He wouldn't know enough about what women wear to do it properly."

"It was queer," said Gwenda. "In his office that day. I had an odd sort of feeling that he was like a house with its blinds pulled down . . . and I even had a fanciful idea that —that there was someone dead in the house."

She looked at Miss Marple.

"Does that seem very silly to you?" she asked.

"No, my dear. I think that perhaps you were right."

"And now," said Gwenda, "we come to Afflick. Afflick's Tours. Jackie Afflick who was always too smart by half. The first thing against him is that Dr. Kennedy believed he had incipient persecution mania. That is—he was never really normal. He's told us about himself and Helen—but we'll agree now that that was all a pack of lies. He didn't just think she was a cute kid—he was madly, passionately in love with her. But she wasn't in love with him. She was just amusing herself. She was man mad, as Miss Marple says."

"No, dear, *I* didn't say that. Nothing of the kind."

"Well, a nymphomaniac, if you prefer the term. Anyway, she had an affair with Jackie Afflick and then wanted to drop him. He didn't want to be dropped. Her brother got her out of her scrape, but Jackie Afflick never forgave or forgot. He lost his job—according to him through being framed by Walter Fane. That shows definite signs of persecution mania."

"Yes," agreed Giles. "But on the other hand, if it was true, it's another point against Fane —quite a valuable point."

Gwenda went on.

"Helen goes abroad, and he leaves Dillmouth. But he never forgets her, and when she returns to Dillmouth, married, he comes over and visits her. He said first of all, he came *once*, but later on, he admits that he came more than once. And, oh, Giles, don't you remember? Edith Pagett used a phrase about 'our mystery man in a flashy car.' You see, he came often enough to make the servants talk. But Helen took pains not to ask him to a meal—not to let him meet Kelvin. Perhaps she was afraid of him. Perhaps—"

Giles interrupted.

"This might cut both ways. Supposing Helen was in love with him—the first man she ever was in love with, and supposing she went on being in love with him. Perhaps they had an affair together and she didn't let anyone know about it. But perhaps he wanted her to go away with him, and by that time she was tired of him, and wouldn't go, and so—and so—he killed her. And all the rest of it. Lily said in her letter to Dr. Kennedy there was a posh car standing outside that night. It was Jackie Afflick's car. Jackie Afflick was 'on the spot,' too.

"It's an assumption," said Giles. "But it seems to me a reasonable one. But there are Helen's letters to be worked into our reconstruction. I've been puzzling my brains to think of the 'circumstances,' as Miss Marple put it, under which she could have been induced to write those letters. It seems to me that to explain them, we've got to admit that she actually *had* a lover, and that she was expecting to go away with him. We'll test our three possibles again. Erskine first. Say that he still wasn't prepared to leave his wife or break up his home, but that Helen had agreed to leave Kelvin Halliday and go somewhere where Erskine could come and be with her from time to time. The first thing would be to disarm Mrs. Erskine's suspicions, so Helen writes a couple of letters to reach her brother in due course which will look as though she has gone abroad with someone. That fits in very well with her being so mysterious about who the man in question is."

"But if she was going to leave her husband for him, why did he kill her?" asked Gwenda.

"Perhaps because she suddenly changed her mind. Decided that she did really care for her husband after all. He just saw red and strangled her. Then he took the clothes and suitcase and used the letters. That's a perfectly good explanation covering everything."

"The same might apply to Walter Fane. I should imagine that scandal might be absolutely disastrous to a country solicitor. Helen might have agreed to go somewhere nearby where Fane could visit her but pretend that she had gone abroad with someone else.

Letters all prepared and then, as you suggested, she changed her mind. Walter went mad and killed her."

"What about Jackie Afflick?"

"It's more difficult to find a reason for the letters with him. I shouldn't imagine that scandal would affect him. Perhaps Helen was afraid, not of him, but of my father—and so thought it would be better to pretend she'd gone abroad—or perhaps Afflick's wife had the money at that time, and he wanted her money to invest in his business. Oh yes, there are lots of possibilities for the letters."

"Which one do you fancy, Miss Marple?" asked Gwenda. "I don't really think Walter Fane—but then—"

Mrs. Cocker had just come in to clear away the coffee cups.

"There now, madam," she said. "I quite forgot. All this about a poor woman being murdered and you and Mr. Reed mixed up in it, not at all the right thing for you, madam, just now. Mr. Fane was here this afternoon, asking for you. He waited quite half an hour. Seemed to think you were expecting him."

"How strange," said Gwenda. "What time?"

"It must have been about four o'clock or just after. And then, after that, there was another gentleman, came in a great big yellow car. He was positive you were expecting him. Wouldn't take no for an answer. Waited twenty minutes. I wondered if you'd had some idea of a tea party and forgotten it."

"No," said Gwenda. "How odd."

"Let's ring up Fane now," said Giles. "He won't have gone to bed."

He suited the action to the word.

"Hullo, is that Fane speaking? Giles Reed here. I hear you came round to see us this afternoon—what?—no—no, I'm sure of it—no, how very odd. Yes, I wonder, too."

He laid down the receiver.

"Here's an odd thing. He was rung up in his office this morning. A message left would he come round and see us this afternoon. It was very important."

Giles and Gwenda stared at each other. Then Gwenda said:

"Ring up Afflick."

Again Giles went to the telephone, found the number and rang through. It took a little longer, but presently he got the connection.

"Mr. Afflick? Giles Reed, I—"

Here he was obviously interrupted by a flow of speech from the other end.

At last he was able to say:

"But we didn't—no—I assure you—nothing of the kind. Yes—yes, I know you're a busy man. I wouldn't have dreamed of—Yes, but look here, who was it rang you—a man?—no, I tell you it wasn't me. No—no, I see. Well, I agree, it's quite extraordinary."

He replaced the receiver and came back to the table.

"Well, there it is," he said. "Somebody, a man who said he was me, rang up Afflick and asked him to come over here. It was urgent—big sum of money involved."

They looked at each other.

"It could have been either of them," said Gwenda. "Don't you see, Giles? Either of them could have killed Lily and come on here as an alibi."

"Hardly an alibi, dear," put in Miss Marple.

"I don't mean quite an alibi, but an excuse for being away from their office. What I mean is, one of them is speaking the truth and one is lying. One of them rang up the other and asked him to come here—to throw suspicion on him—but we don't know which. It's a clear issue now between the two of them. Fane or Afflick. I say—Jackie Afflick."

"I think Walter Fane," said Giles.

They both looked at Miss Marple.

She shook her head.

"There's another possibility," she said.

"Of course, Erskine."

Giles fairly ran across to the telephone.

"What are you going to do?" asked Gwenda.

"Put through a trunk call to Northumberland."

"Oh, Giles—you can't really think—"

"We've got to know. If he's there—he can't have killed Lily Kimble this afternoon. No private aeroplanes or silly stuff like that."

They waited in silence until the telephone bell rang.

Giles picked up the receiver.

"You were asking for a personal call to Major Erskine. Go ahead, please. Major Erskine is waiting."

Clearing his throat nervously, Giles said:

"Er—Erskine? Giles Reed here—Reed, yes."

He cast a sudden agonized glance at Gwenda which said as plainly as possible: "What the hell do I say now?"

Gwenda got up and took the receiver from him.

"Major Erskine? This is Mrs. Reed here. We've heard of—of a house. Linscott Brake. Is—is it—do you know anything about it? It's somewhere near you, I believe."

Erskine's voice said:

"Linscott Brake? No, I don't think I've ever heard of it. What's the postal town?"

"It's terribly blurred," said Gwenda. "You know those awful typescripts agents send out. But it says fifteen miles from Daith, so we thought—"

"I'm sorry. I haven't heard of it. Who lives there?"

"Oh, it's empty. But never mind, actually

we've—we've practically settled on a house. I'm so sorry to have bothered you. I expect you were busy."

"No, not at all. At least only busy domestically. My wife's away. And our cook had to go off to her mother, so I've been dealing with domestic routine. I'm afraid I'm not much of a hand at it. Better in the garden."

"I'd always rather do gardening than housework. I hope your wife isn't ill?"

"Oh no, she was called away to a sister. She'll be back tomorrow."

"Well, good night, and so sorry to have bothered you."

She put down the receiver.

"Erskine is out of it," she said triumphantly. "His wife's away and he's doing all the chores. So that leaves it between the two others. Doesn't it, Miss Marple?"

Miss Marple was looking grave.

"I don't think, my dears," she said, "that you have given quite enough thought to the matter. Oh, dear—I am really very worried. If only I knew exactly what to do. . . ."

24

The Monkey's Paws

Gwenda leaned her elbows on the table and cupped her chin in them while her eyes roamed dispassionately over the remains of a hasty lunch. Presently she must deal with them, carry them out to the scullery, wash up, put things away, see what there would be, later, for supper.

But there was no wild hurry. She felt she needed a little time to take things in. Everything had been happening too fast.

The events of the morning, when she reviewed them, seemed to be chaotic and impossible. Everything had happened too quickly and too improbably.

Inspector Last had appeared early—at half-past nine. With him had come Detective Inspector Primer from headquarters and the Chief Constable of the county. The latter had not stayed long. It was Inspector Primer who was now in charge of the case of Lily Kimble deceased and all the ramifications arising therefrom.

It was Inspector Primer, a man with a deceptively mild manner and a gentle, apologetic voice, who had asked her if it would inconvenience her very much if his men did some digging in the garden.

From the tone of his voice, it might have been a case of giving his men some healthful exercise, rather than of seeking for a dead body which had been buried for eighteen years.

Giles had spoken up then. He had said:

"I think, perhaps, we could help you with a suggestion or two."

And he told the Inspector about the shifting of the steps leading down to the lawn, and took the Inspector out onto the terrace.

The Inspector had looked up at the barred window on the first floor at the corner of the house and had said:

"That would be the nursery, I presume."

And Giles said that it would.

Then the Inspector and Giles had come back into the house, and two men with spades had gone out into the garden, and Giles, before the Inspector could get down to questions, had said:

"I think, Inspector, you had better hear something that my wife has so far not mentioned to anyone except myself—and—er—one other person."

The gentle, rather compelling gaze of Inspector Primer came to rest on Gwenda. It was faintly speculative. He was asking himself, Gwenda thought: "Is this a woman who can be depended upon, or is she the kind who imagines things?"

So strongly did she feel this, that she started in a defensive way:

"I may have imagined it. Perhaps I did. But it seems awfully real."

Inspector Primer said softly and soothingly:

"Well, Mrs. Reed, let's hear about it."

And Gwenda had explained. How the house had seemed familiar to her when she first saw it. How she had subsequently learned that she had, in fact, lived there as a child. How she had remembered the nursery wallpaper, and the connecting door, and the feeling she had had that there ought to be steps down to the lawn.

Inspector Primer nodded. He did not say that Gwenda's childish recollections were not particularly interesting, but Gwenda wondered whether he were thinking it.

Then she nerved herself to the final statement. How she had suddenly remembered, when sitting at a theatre, looking through the banisters at Hillside and seeing a dead woman in the hall.

"With a blue face, strangled, and golden hair—and it was Helen— But it was so stupid, I didn't know at all who Helen *was*."

"We think that—" Giles began, but Inspector Primer, with unexpected authority, held up an arresting hand.

"Please let Mrs. Reed tell me in her own words."

And Gwenda had stumbled on, her face flushed, with Inspector Primer gently helping her out, using a dexterity that Gwenda did not appreciate as the highly technical performance it was.

"Webster?" he said thoughtfully. "H'm, *Duchess of Malfi*. Monkey's paws?"

"But that was probably a nightmare," said Giles.

"Please, Mr. Reed."

"It may all have been a nightmare," said Gwenda.

"No, I don't think it was," said Inspector Primer. "It would be very hard to explain Lily Kimble's death, unless we assume that there *was* a woman murdered in this house."

That seemed so reasonable and almost comforting that Gwenda hurried on.

"And it wasn't my father who murdered her. It wasn't really. Even Dr. Penrose says he wasn't the right type, and that he couldn't have murdered anybody. And Dr. Kennedy was quite sure he hadn't done it, but only thought he had. So you see it was someone who wanted it to *seem* as though my father had done it, and we think we know who— at least it's one of two people—"

"Gwenda," said Giles. "We can't really—"

"I wonder, Mr. Reed," said the Inspector, "if you would mind going out into the garden and seeing how my men are getting on. Tell them I sent you."

He closed the French windows after Giles and latched them and came back to Gwenda.

"Now just tell me all your ideas, Mrs. Reed. Never mind if they are rather incoherent."

And Gwenda had poured out all hers and Giles's speculations and reasonings, and the steps they had taken to find out all they could about the three men who might have figured in Helen Halliday's life, and the final conclusions they had come to—and how both Walter Fane and J. J. Afflick had been rung up, as though by Giles, and had been summoned to Hillside the preceding afternoon.

"But you do see, don't you, Inspector—that one of them might be lying?"

And in a gentle, rather tired voice, the Inspector said:

"That's one of the principal difficulties in my kind of work. So many people may be lying. And so many people usually are . . . though not always for the reasons that you'd think. And some people don't even know they're lying."

"Do you think I'm like that?" Gwenda asked apprehensively.

And the Inspector smiled and said:

"I think you're a very truthful witness, Mrs. Reed."

"And you think I'm right about who murdered her?"

The Inspector sighed and said:

"It's not a question of thinking—not with us. It's a question of checking up. Where everybody was, what account everybody gives of their movements. We know accurately enough, to within ten minutes or so, when Lily Kimble was killed. Between two-twenty and two forty-five. Anyone could have killed her and then come on here yesterday afternoon. I don't see, myself, any reason for those telephone calls. It doesn't give either of the people you mention an alibi for the time of the murder."

"But you will find out, won't you, what they were doing at the time? Between two-twenty and two forty-five. You will ask them."

Inspector Primer smiled.

"We shall ask all the questions necessary, Mrs. Reed, you may be sure of that. All in good time. There's no good in rushing things. You've got to see your way ahead."

Gwenda had a sudden vision of patience and quiet unsensational work. Unhurried, remorseless . . .

She said:

"I see . . . yes. Because you're professional. And Giles and I are just amateurs. We might make a lucky hit—but we wouldn't really know how to follow it up."

"Something of the kind, Mrs. Reed."

The Inspector smiled again. He got up

and unfastened the French windows. Then, just as he was about to step through them, he stopped. Rather, Gwenda thought, like a pointing dog.

"Excuse me, Mrs. Reed. That lady wouldn't be a Miss Jane Marple, would she?"

Gwenda had come to stand beside him. At the bottom of the garden Miss Marple was still waging a losing war with bindweed.

"Yes, that's Miss Marple. She's awfully kind in helping us with the garden."

"Miss Marple," said the Inspector. "I see."

Gwenda looked at him inquiringly and said:

"She's rather a dear."

He replied:

"She's a very celebrated lady, is Miss Marple. Got the Chief Constables of at least three counties in her pocket. She's not got my Chief yet, but I daresay that will come. So Miss Marple's got her finger in this pie."

"She's made an awful lot of helpful suggestions," said Gwenda.

"I bet she has," said the Inspector. "Was it her suggestion where to look for the deceased Mrs. Halliday?"

"She said that Giles and I ought to know quite well where to look," said Gwenda. "And it did seem stupid of us not to have thought of it before."

The Inspector gave a soft little laugh, and

went down to stand by Miss Marple. He said:

"I don't think we've been introduced, Miss Marple. But you were pointed out to me once by Colonel Melrose."

Miss Marple stood up, flushed and grasping a handful of clinging green.

"Oh yes. Dear Colonel Melrose. He has always been *most* kind. Ever since—"

"Ever since a churchwarden was shot in the vicar's study. Quite a while ago. But you've had other successes since then. A little poison pen trouble down near Lymstock."

"You seem to know quite a lot about me, Inspector—"

"Primer, my name is. And you've been busy here, I expect."

"Well, I try to do what I can in the garden. Sadly neglected. This bindweed, for instance, such nasty stuff. Its roots," said Miss Marple, looking very earnestly at the Inspector, "go down underground a long way. A very long way—they run along underneath the soil."

"I think you're right about that," said the Inspector. "A long way down. A long way back . . . this murder, I mean. Eighteen years."

"And perhaps before that," said Miss Marple. "Running underground . . . And terribly harmful, Inspector, squeezing the life out of the pretty growing flowers . . ."

One of the police constables came along the path. He was perspiring and had a smudge of earth on his forehead.

"We've come to—something, sir. Looks as though it's her all right."

II

And it was then, Gwenda reflected, that the nightmarish quality of the day had begun. Giles coming in, his face rather pale, saying: "It's—she's there all right, Gwenda."

Then one of the constables had telephoned and the police surgeon, a short bustling man, had arrived.

And it was then that Mrs. Cocker, the calm and imperturbable Mrs. Cocker, had gone out into the garden—not led, as might have been expected by ghoulish curiosity, but solely in the quest of culinary herbs for the dish she was preparing for lunch. And Mrs. Cocker, whose reaction to the news of a murder on the preceding day had been shocked censure and an anxiety for the effect upon Gwenda's health (for Mrs. Cocker had made up her mind that the nursery upstairs was to be tenanted after the due number of months), had walked straight in upon the gruesome discovery, and had been immediately "taken queer" to an alarming extent.

"Too horrible, madam. Bones is a thing I never could abide. Not skeleton bones, as one might say. And here in the garden, just by the mint and all. And my heart's beating at such a rate—palpitations—I can hardly get my breath. And if I might make so bold, just a thimbleful of brandy . . ."

Alarmed by Mrs. Cocker's gasps and her ashy colour, Gwenda had rushed to the sideboard, poured out some brandy and brought it to Mrs. Cocker to sip.

And Mrs. Cocker had said:

"That's just what I needed, madam—" when, quite suddenly, her voice had failed, and she had looked so alarming that Gwenda had screamed for Giles, and Giles had yelled to the police surgeon.

"And it's fortunate I was on the spot," the latter said afterwards. "It was touch and go anyway. Without a doctor, that woman would have died then and there."

And then Inspector Primer had taken the brandy decanter, and then he and the doctor had gone into a huddle over it, and Inspector Primer had asked Gwenda when she and Giles had last had any brandy out of it.

Gwenda said she thought not for some days. They'd been away—up North, and the last few times they'd had a drink, they'd had gin. "But I nearly had some brandy yesterday," said Gwenda. "Only it makes me think of channel steamers, so Giles opened a new bottle of whisky."

"That was very lucky for you, Mrs. Reed. If you'd drunk brandy yesterday, I doubt if you would be alive today."

"Giles nearly drank some—but in the end he had whisky with me."

Gwenda shivered.

Even now, alone in the house, with the police gone and Giles gone with them after a hasty lunch scratched up out of tins (since Mrs. Cocker had been removed to hospital), Gwenda could hardly believe in the morning turmoil of events.

One thing stood out clearly—the presence in the house yesterday of Jackie Afflick and Walter Fane. Either of them could have tampered with the brandy, and what was the purpose of the telephone calls unless it was to afford one or other of them the opportunity to poison the brandy decanter? Gwenda and Giles had been getting too near the truth. Or had a third person come in from outside, through the open dining-room window perhaps, while she and Giles had been sitting in Dr. Kennedy's house waiting for Lily Kimble to keep her appointment? A third person who had engineered the telephone calls to steer suspicion on the other two?

But a third person, Gwenda thought, didn't make sense. For a third person, surely, would have telephoned to only *one* of the two men. A third person would have wanted one suspect, not two. And anyway, who could the third person be? Erskine had definitely been in Northumberland. No, either Walter Fane had telephoned to Afflick and had pretended to be telephoned to himself. Or else Afflick had telephoned Fane, and had made the same pretence of receiving a summons. One of those two, and the police, who were cleverer and had more resources than she and Giles had, would find out which. And in the meantime both of those men would be watched. They wouldn't be able to—to try again.

Again Gwenda shivered. It took a little getting used to—the knowledge that someone had tried to kill you. "Dangerous," Miss Marple had said long ago. But she and Giles had not really taken the idea of danger seriously. Even after Lily Kimble had been killed, it still hadn't occurred to her that anyone would try and kill her and Giles. Just because she and Giles were getting too near the truth of what had happened eighteen years ago. Working out what must have happened then—and who had made it happen.

Walter Fane and Jackie Afflick ...

"Which?"

Gwenda closed her eyes, seeing them afresh in the light of her new knowledge.

Quiet Walter Fane, sitting in his office— the pale spider in the centre of its web. So quiet, so harmless-looking. A house with its blinds down. Someone dead in the house. Someone dead eighteen years ago—but still there. How sinister the quiet Walter Fane seemed now. Walter Fane, who had once flung himself murderously upon his brother.

Walter Fane, whom Helen had scornfully refused to marry, once here at home, and once again in India. A double rebuff. A double ignominy. Walter Fane, so quiet, so unemotional, who could express himself, perhaps, only in sudden murderous violence —as, possibly, quiet Lizzie Borden had once done. . . .

Gwenda opened her eyes. She had convinced herself, hadn't she, that Walter Fane was the man.

One might, perhaps, just consider Afflick. With eyes open, not shut.

His loud check suit, his domineering manner—just the opposite to Walter Fane— nothing repressed or quiet about Afflick. But possibly he had put that manner on because of an inferiority complex. It worked that way, experts said. If you weren't sure of yourself, you had to boast and assert yourself and be overbearing. Turned down by Helen because he wasn't good enough for her. The sore festering, not forgotten. Determination to get on in the world. Persecution. Everyone against him. Discharged from his employment by a faked charge made up by an "enemy." Surely that did show that Afflick wasn't normal. And what a feeling of power a man like that would get out of killing. That good-natured jovial face of his, it was a cruel face really. He was a cruel man—and his thin pale wife knew it and was afraid of him. Lily Kimble had threatened him and Lily

Kimble had died. Gwenda and Giles had interfered—then Gwenda and Giles must die, too, and he would involve Walter Fane, who had sacked him long ago. That fitted in very nicely.

Gwenda shook herself, came out of her imaginings, and returned to practicality. Giles would be home and want his tea. She must clear away and wash up lunch.

She fetched a tray and took the things out to the kitchen. Everything in the kitchen was exquisitely neat. Mrs. Cocker was really a treasure.

By the side of the sink was a pair of surgical rubber gloves. Mrs. Cocker always wore a pair for washing up. Her niece, who worked in a hospital, got them at a reduced price.

Gwenda fitted them on over her hands and began to wash up the dishes. She might as well keep her hands nice.

She washed the plates and put them in the rack, washed and dried the other things, and put everything neatly away.

Then, still lost in thought, she went upstairs. She might as well, she thought, wash out those stockings and a jumper or two. She'd keep the gloves on.

These things were in the forefront of her mind. But somewhere, underneath them, something was nagging at her.

Walter Fane or Jackie Afflick, she had said. One or the other of them. And she had made out quite a good case against either of them. Perhaps that was what really worried her. Because, strictly speaking, it would be much more satisfactory if you could only make out a good case against *one* of them. One ought to be sure, by now, *which*. And Gwenda wasn't sure.

If only there was someone else . . . But there couldn't be anyone else. Because Richard Erskine was out of it. Richard Erskine had been in Northumberland when Lily Kimble was killed and when the brandy in the decanter had been tampered with. Yes, Richard Erskine was right out of it.

She was glad of that, because she liked Richard Erskine. Richard Erskine was attractive—very attractive. How sad for him to be married to that megalith of a woman with her suspicious eyes and deep bass voice. Just like a man's voice . . .

Like a man's voice . . .

The idea flashed through her mind with a queer misgiving. . . .

A man's voice . . . Could it have been Mrs. Erskine, not her husband, who had replied to Giles on the telephone last night?

No—no, surely not. No, of course not. She and Giles would have known. And anyway, to begin with, Mrs. Erskine could have had no idea of who was ringing up. No, of course it was Erskine speaking, and his wife, as he said, was away.

His wife was away . . .

Surely—no, that was impossible. . . . Could

it have been *Mrs.* Erskine? Mrs. Erskine, driven insane by jealousy? Mrs. Erskine, to whom Lily Kimble had written? Was it a *woman* Leonie had seen in the garden that night when she looked out of the window?

There was a sudden bang in the hall below. Somebody had come in through the front door.

Gwenda came out from the bathroom onto the landing and looked over the banisters. She was relieved to see it was Dr. Kennedy. She called down:

"I'm here."

Her hands were held out in front of her—wet, glistening, a queer pinkish grey—they reminded her of something. . . .

Kennedy looked up, shading his eyes.

"Is that you, Gwennie? I can't see your face. . . . My eyes are dazzled—"

And then Gwenda screamed. . . .

Looking at those smooth monkey's paws and hearing that voice in the hall—

"It was you . . ." she gasped. "You killed her . . . killed Helen . . . I—know now. It was you . . . all along. . . . You . . ."

He came up the stairs towards her—slowly—looking up at her.

"Why couldn't you leave me alone?" he said. "Why did you have to meddle? Why did you have to bring—her—back? Just when I'd begun to forget—to forget . . . You brought her back again—Helen—my Helen. Bringing it all up again. I had to kill Lily—now

I'll have to kill you. Like I killed Helen . . . Yes, like I killed Helen . . ."

He was close upon her now—his hands out towards her—reaching, she knew, for her throat. That kind quizzical face—that nice ordinary, elderly face—the same still, but for the eyes—the eyes were not sane. . . .

Gwenda retreated before him slowly, the scream frozen in her throat. She had screamed once. She could not scream again. And if she did scream, no one would hear.

Because there was no one in the house— not Giles, and not Mrs. Cocker, not even Miss Marple in the garden. Nobody. And the house next door was too far away to hear if she screamed. And anyway, she couldn't scream. . . . Because she was too frightened to scream. Frightened of those horrible reaching hands . . .

She could back away and he would follow her until she stood there with her back to the nursery door and then—and then—those hands would fasten round her throat. . . .

A pitiful little stifled whimper came from between her lips . . .

And then, suddenly, Dr. Kennedy stopped and reeled back as a jet of soapy water struck him between the eyes. He gasped and blinked and his hands went to his face.

"So fortunate," said Miss Marple's voice, rather breathless, for she had run violently up the back stairs, "that I was just syringing the greenfly off your roses. . . ."

25

Postscript at Torquay

"But, of course, dear Gwenda, I should never have dreamed of going away and leaving you alone in the house," said Miss Marple. "I knew there was a very dangerous person at large, and I was keeping an unobtrusive watch from the garden."

"Did you know it was—him—all along?" asked Gwenda.

They were all three—Miss Marple, Gwenda and Giles—sitting on the terrace of the Imperial Hotel at Torquay.

"A change of scene," Miss Marple had said and Giles had agreed, would be the best thing for Gwenda. So Inspector Primer had concurred and they had driven to Torquay forthwith.

Miss Marple said in answer to Gwenda's question:

"Well, he did seem indicated, my dear. Although unfortunately there was nothing in the way of evidence to go upon. Just indications, nothing more."

Looking at her curiously, Giles said:

"But I can't see any indications even."

"Oh, dear Giles, think. He was *on the spot*, to begin with."

"On the spot?"

"But certainly. When Kelvin Halliday came to him that night he *had just come back from the hospital*. And the hospital, at that time, as several people told us, was actually next door to Hillside, or St. Catherine's, as it was then called. So that, as you see, puts him in *the right place at the right time*. And then there were a hundred and one little significant facts. Helen Halliday told Richard Erskine she had gone out to marry Walter Fane because *she wasn't happy at home*. Not happy, that is, living with her brother. Yet her brother was by all accounts devoted to her. So why wasn't she happy? Mr. Afflick told you that he 'was sorry for the poor kid.' I think that he was absolutely truthful when he said that. He was sorry for her. Why did she have to go and meet young Afflick in that clandestine way? Admittedly she was not wildly in love with him. Was it because she couldn't meet young men in the ordinary normal way? Her brother was 'strict' and 'old-fashioned.' It is vaguely reminiscent, is it not, of Mr. Barrett of Wimpole Street?"

Gwenda shivered.

"He was mad," she said. "Mad."

"Yes," said Miss Marple. "He wasn't normal. He adored his half-sister, and that affection became possessive and unwholesome. That kind of thing happens oftener than you'd think. Fathers who don't want their daughters to marry—or even to meet young men. Like Mr. Barrett. I thought of that when I heard about the tennis net."

"The tennis net?"

"Yes, that seemed to me very significant. Think of that girl, young Helen, coming home from school, and eager for all a young girl wants out of life, anxious to meet young men—to flirt with them—"

"A little sex crazy."

"*No*," said Miss Marple with emphasis. "*That* is one of the wickedest things about this crime. Dr. Kennedy didn't only kill her physically. If you think back carefully, you'll see that the only evidence for Helen Kennedy's having been man mad or practically—what is the word you used, dear?—oh yes, a nymphomaniac, came actually from *Dr. Kennedy* himself. I think, myself, that she was a perfectly normal young girl who wanted to have fun and a good time and flirt a little and finally settle down with the man of her choice—no more than that. And see what steps her brother took. First he was strict and old-fashioned about allowing her liberty. Then, when she wanted to give tennis parties—a most normal and harmless desire—he pretended to agree and then one night secretly cut the tennis net to ribbons— a very significant and sadistic action. Then, since she could still go out to play tennis or to dances, he took advantage of a grazed foot which he treated, to infect it so that it wouldn't heal. Oh yes, I think he did that . . . in fact, I'm sure of it.

"Mind you, I don't think Helen realized any of all this. She knew her brother had a deep affection for her and I don't think she knew *why* she felt uneasy and unhappy at home. But she did feel like that and at last she decided to go out to India and marry young Fane simply in order to get away. To get away from *what*? She didn't know. She was too young and guileless to know. So she went off to India and on the way she met Richard Erskine and fell in love with him. There again, she behaved not like a sex-crazy girl, but like a decent and honourable girl. She didn't urge him to leave his wife. She urged him not to do so. But when she saw Walter Fane, she knew that she couldn't marry him, and because she didn't know what else to do, she wired her brother for money to go home.

"On the way home she met your father— and another way of escape showed itself.

This time it was one with good prospects of happiness.

"She didn't marry your father under false pretences, Gwenda. He was recovering from the death of a dearly loved wife. She was getting over an unhappy love affair. They could both help each other. I think it is significant that she and Kelvin Halliday were married in London and then went down to Dillmouth to break the news to Dr. Kennedy. She must have had some instinct that that would be a wiser thing to do than to go down and be married in Dillmouth, which ordinarily would have been the normal thing to do. I still think she didn't know what she was up against—but she was uneasy, and she felt safer in presenting her brother with the marriage as a *fait accompli*.

"Kelvin Halliday was very friendly to Kennedy and liked him. Kennedy seems to have gone out of his way to appear pleased about the marriage. The couple took a furnished house there.

"And now we come to that very significant fact—the suggestion that Kelvin was being drugged by his wife. There are only two possible explanations of that—because there are only two people who could have had the opportunity of doing such a thing. Either Helen Halliday *was* drugging her husband, and if so, why? Or else the drugs were being administered by Dr. Kennedy. Kennedy was Halliday's physician, as is clear by Halliday's consulting him. He had confidence in Kennedy's medical knowledge—and the suggestion that his wife was drugging him was very cleverly suggested to him by Kennedy."

"But could any drug make a man have the hallucination that he was strangling his wife?" asked Giles. "I mean there isn't any drug, is there, that has that particular effect?"

"My dear Giles, you've fallen into the trap again—the trap of believing *what is said to you*. There is only Dr. Kennedy's word for it that Halliday ever had *that* hallucination. He himself never says so in his diary. He had hallucinations, yes, but he does not mention their nature. But I daresay Kennedy talked to him about men who had strangled their wives after passing through a phase such as Kelvin Halliday was experiencing."

"Dr. Kennedy was really wicked," said Gwenda.

"I think," said Miss Marple, "that he'd definitely passed the border line between sanity and madness by that time. And Helen, poor girl, began to realize it. It was to her brother she must have been speaking that day when she was overheard by Lily. 'I think I've always been afraid of you.' That was one of the things she said. And that always was very significant. And so she determined to leave Dillmouth. She persuaded her husband to buy a house in Norfolk, she persuaded him not to tell anyone about it. That in itself, you know, was a very curious point. The secrecy about it was very illuminating. She was clearly very afraid of *someone* knowing about it—but that did not fit in with the Walter Fane theory or the Jackie Afflick theory—and certainly not with Richard Erskine's being concerned. No, it pointed to somewhere much nearer home.

"And in the end, Kelvin Halliday, whom doubtless the secrecy irked and who felt it to be pointless, told his brother-in-law.

"And in doing so, sealed his own fate and that of his wife. For Kennedy was not going to let Helen go and live happily with her husband. I think perhaps his idea was simply to break down Halliday's health with drugs. But at the revelation that his victim and Helen were going to escape him, he became completely unhinged. From the hospital he went through into the garden of St. Catherine's and he took with him a pair of surgical gloves. He caught Helen in the hall, and he strangled her. Nobody saw him, there was no one there to see him, or so he thought, and so, racked with love and frenzy, he quoted those tragic lines that were so apposite."

Miss Marple sighed and clucked her tongue.

"I was stupid—very stupid. We were all

stupid. We should have seen at once. Those lines from *The Duchess of Malfi* were really the clue to the whole thing. They are said, are they not, by a *brother* who has just contrived his sister's death to avenge her marriage to the man she loved. Yes, we were stupid—"

"And then?" asked Giles.

"And then he went through with the whole devilish plan. The body carried upstairs. The clothes packed in a suitcase. A note written and thrown in the waste-paper basket to convince Halliday later."

"But I should have thought," said Gwenda, "that it would have been better from his point of view for my father actually to have been convicted of the murder."

Miss Marple shook her head.

"Oh no, he couldn't risk that. He had a lot of shrewd Scottish common sense, you know. He had a wholesome respect for the police. The police take a lot of convincing before they believe a man guilty of murder. The police might have asked a lot of awkward questions and made a lot of awkward inquiries as to times and places. No, his plan was simpler and, I think, more devilish. He only had Halliday to convince. First, that he had killed his wife. Secondly that he was mad. He persuaded Halliday to go into a mental home, but I don't think he really wanted to convince him that it was all a delusion. Your father accepted that theory, Gwennie, mainly, I should imagine, for your sake. He continued to believe that he had killed Helen. He died believing that."

"Wicked," said Gwenda. "Wicked—wicked —wicked."

"Yes," said Miss Marple. "There isn't really any other word. And I think, Gwenda, that that is why your childish impression of what you saw remained so strong. It was real evil that was in the air that night."

"But the letters," said Giles. "Helen's letters? They *were* in her handwriting, so they couldn't be forgeries."

"Of course they were forgeries! But that is where he overreached himself. He was so anxious, you see, to stop you and Gwenda making investigations. He could probably imitate Helen's handwriting quite nicely— but it wouldn't fool an expert. So the sample of Helen's handwriting he sent you with the letter wasn't her handwriting either. He wrote it himself. So naturally it tallied."

"Goodness," said Giles. "I never thought of that."

"No," said Miss Marple. "You believed what he said. It really is very dangerous to believe people. *I* never have for years."

"And the brandy?"

"He did that the day he came to Hillside with Helen's letter and talked to me in the garden. He was waiting in the house while Mrs. Cocker came out and told me he was there. It would only take a minute."

"Good Lord," said Giles. "And he urged me to take Gwenda home and give her brandy after we were at the police station when Lily Kimble was killed. How did he arrange to meet her earlier?"

"That was very simple. The original letter he sent her asked her to meet him at Woodleigh Camp and come to Matchings Halt by the two-o-five train from Dillmouth Junction. He came out of the copse of trees, probably, and accosted her as she was going up the lane—and strangled her. Then he simply substituted the letter you all saw for the letter she had with her (and which he had asked her to bring because of the directions in it) and went home to prepare for you and play out the little comedy of waiting for Lily."

"And Lily really was threatening him? Her letter didn't sound as though she was. Her letter sounded as though she suspected Afflick."

"Perhaps she did. But Leonie, the Swiss girl, had talked to Lily, and Leonie was the one danger to Kennedy. Because she looked out of the nursery window and saw him digging in the garden. In the morning he talked to her, told her bluntly that Major Halliday had killed his wife—that Major Halliday was insane, and that he, Kennedy, was hush-ing up the matter for the child's sake. If, however, Leonie felt she ought to go to the police, she must do so, but it would be very unpleasant for her—and so on.

"Leonie took immediate fright at the mention of the police. She adored you and had implicit faith in what monsieur le docteur thought best. Kennedy paid her a handsome sum of money and hustled her back to Switzerland. But before she went, she hinted something to Lily as to your father's having killed his wife and that she had seen the body buried. That fitted in with Lily's ideas at the time. She took it for granted it was Kelvin Halliday that Leonie had seen digging the grave."

"But Kennedy didn't know that, of course," said Giles.

"Of course not. When he got Lily's letter, the words in it that frightened him were that Leonie had told Lily what she had seen *out of the window* and the mention of the car outside."

"The car? Jackie Afflick's car?"

"Another misunderstanding. Lily remembered, or thought she remembered, a car like Jackie Afflick's being outside in the road. Already her imagination had got to work on the mystery man who came over to see Mrs. Halliday. With the hospital next door, no doubt a good many cars did park along this road. But you must remember that the *doc-*

tor's car was actually standing outside the hospital that night—he probably leaped to the conclusion that she meant *his* car. The adjective *posh* was meaningless to him."

"I see," said Giles. "Yes, to a guilty conscience that letter of Lily's might look like blackmail. But how do you know all about Leonie?"

Her lips pursed close together, Miss Marple said:

"He went—right over the edge, you know. As soon as the men Inspector Primer had left rushed in and seized him. He went over the whole crime again and again—everything he'd done. Leonie died, it seems, very shortly after her return to Switzerland. Overdose of some sleeping tablets. . . . Oh no, he wasn't taking any chances."

"Like trying to poison me with the brandy."

"You were very dangerous to him, you and Giles. Fortunately you never told him about your memory of seeing Helen dead in the hall. He never knew there had been an eyewitness."

"Those telephone calls to Fane and Afflick," said Giles. "Did he put those through?"

"Yes. If there was an inquiry as to who could have tampered with the brandy, either of them would make an admirable suspect, and if Jackie Afflick drove over in his car alone, it might tie him in with Lily Kimble's murder. Fane would most likely have an alibi."

"And he seemed fond of me," said Gwenda. "Little Gwennie."

"He had to play his part," said Miss Marple. "Imagine what it meant to him. After eighteen years, you and Giles come along, asking questions, burrowing into the past, disturbing a murder that had seemed dead but was only sleeping. . . . Murder in retrospect. . . . A horribly dangerous thing to do, my dears. I have been sadly worried."

"Poor Mrs. Cocker," said Gwenda. "She had a terribly near escape. I'm glad she's going to be all right. Do you think she'll ever come back to us. Giles? After all this?"

"She will if there's a nursery," said Giles gravely, and Gwenda blushed, and Miss Marple smiled a little and looked out across Torquay.

"How very odd it was that it should happen the way it did," mused Gwenda. "My having those rubber gloves on, and looking at them, and then his coming into the hall and saying those words that sounded so like the others. 'Face' . . . and then: 'Eyes dazzled'—"

She shuddered.

"*Cover her face; mine eyes dazzle: she died young* . . . that might have been me . . . if Miss Marple hadn't been there."

She paused and said softly:

"Poor Helen . . . poor lovely Helen . . . who died young. . . . You know, Giles, she isn't there any more—in the house—in the hall. . . . I could feel that yesterday before we left. . . . There's just the house. And the house is fond of us. We can go back if we like. . . ."